Cupid's arrow hit Caleb's heart at an early age, linking him to Millie, the girl he's loved since kindergarten. But when Millie breaks up with him three weeks before high school graduation and marries someone else, Caleb's heart is ripped to pieces.

Caleb swears off long-term relationships and plans to remain a confirmed bachelor. While he's happy to date, he no longer has marriage on his bucket list. He's content with his life, but it suddenly veers off course when not one but two women — his ex and his next — cross his path, threatening his peace and throwing him for a loop. One of them is Millie, a recent and available widow. The other the infamous Jolene.

Caleb faces three paths — secure bachelorhood, a new woman, or an old flame. He can continue to play it safe, and if he does, nothing changes. But if he plays with fire, he risks burning his bridges. Can he take the leap into love or keep the status quo?

Mountain Bachelor
Copyright © 2022 Kathy Kalmar
ISBN: 978-1-4874-3336-9
Cover art by Martine Jardin

Published by eXtasy Books Inc.

Look for us online at:
www.eXtasybooks.com or www.devinedestinies.com

# Mountain Bachelor
## Mountain Series 16

By

Kathy Kalmar

# Dedication

*Larry: Yesterday, today, tomorrow, and Forever*

## In Memoriam

*Linda and Ron Wilson. Oh how I miss you both. Your love and support I can still feel.*

## In Acknowledgement

*Carolynn Gilbreath, my partner in crime. Jay Austin, Editor in Chief for making my dream come true, Bri, for polishing my words, Debbie Nygaard, amazing editor and more, Martine Jardin, artist, The Greater Detroit Romance Writers, Doug Marple, webmaster, and you, my fans.*

## Disclaimer

*The Storm of the Century happened in 1993. I manipulated the date by ten years and fictionalized Mount LeConte Lodge for dramatic purposes.*
*I tried to respectfully imitate the Appalachian English used throughout the south.*
*As always, any mistakes are mine and mine alone.*

# PROLOGUE: THE MAKING OF A MUSIC MAN

1950

Hettie Weathers walked through the yard to the chicken coop, holding her eighteen-month-old son by the hand. Together they reached beneath the broody hens to gather the warm brown eggs. She taught him how to get them without breaking any. Soon the boy was distracted by fluffy chicks, so she was able to place the eggs in the flour sack apron tied around her waist.

They walked back to their cabin, and she placed the eggs in the pie keep.

Her little boy played at her feet, and when she glanced down, her breath caught in her throat. A tick had landed on her son's head! With a strangled cry, she lifted him into her arms and rushed out the door and down the hollow as fast as she could until she reached Uncle Lem's cabin. She burst through the door and spoke in a rush. "I need Uncle Lem's bow right quick!"

Auntie Bett put her hand over her thin chest. "Lawd, girl, y'all did give me a start! What put a bee in yer bonnet? I'm a-gittin it." She took care to place the fiddle bow in Hettie's hand.

Hettie knelt beside her tiny boy so as not to spook him, then pinched off the plump, red-brown tick fattening itself on

1

Caleb. The tick stuck plumb up in Caleb's head as it sucked the tot's lifeblood. She swiped up the blood using the bow's catgut strings, allowing Caleb's blood droplet to dry on the bowstrings.

Hettie made no attempt to clean the strings. She knew better than to do that.

The wise granny women in the area claimed the blood *must* dry on the strings — not his head — to prevent the dreaded fever. To be a granny woman, one had to be wise and see into both the past and the future with a firm foot in the present. Magic and lore filled mountain life as the people — isolated by geography — had to fend for themselves and make sense out of life and the world surrounding them. Myth, magic, and legend helped them cope.

Then, relieved, she sat back on her heel and fanned her face. She put her finger — wet with her tears — on the bite to stop the blood, knowing a mother's tears could seal and heal the wound. There was nothing else on earth as strong as a mother's tears, or so they said.

Auntie Bett peered at the bite. "That be his first tick bite, right?"

Hettie, still gathering herself, nodded. "Reckon now he'll become a fiddler man."

Old Auntie Bett nodded. "That he will. Pry be the best music man in Sevier County, iffen Uncle Lem learns him."

Auntie Bett walked over to a hand-hewed wooden chest. The trunk creaked when she lifted the top to rummage through several layers of cotton batting. A smile creased her face when she withdrew the trunk's treasure, a pint-sized fiddle. "Y'all be needin' this fair soon."

Hettie smiled and nodded.

Caleb picked it up and plucked a string. Uncle Lem, no doubt drawn by the sound, returned from wherever he was —

the outhouse perhaps — and gave Caleb his first lesson.

The child was a natural, and they all swore he played *Hot Cross Buns* after hearing it only once. Hettie was right proud of her young'un, and her Caleb was plumb smitten with the fiddle.

# CHAPTER ONE: STOP IN THE NAME OF LOVE

March 1969

The spring breeze tickled the treetops and kissed Millie Maples' hot face. She felt the caress of air was a blessin' on their lovin', full of promises of delights to follow.

*Wait, what am I thinkin'?* "Stop! Caleb, that's far enough," Millie said mid-pant. "You promised. We're breaking our rule."

She could barely stop herself, so slowing Caleb Weathers down was a feat in itself—like stopping a speeding bullet from a long gun.

Caleb halted but with obvious difficulty. He groaned and tried to put his penis back inside his jeans as best he could, but not before he ejaculated all over her girlie parts.

He crab-walked away and moaned, "Sorry 'bout that. I reckon yer right. That was way too close for comfort. I got carried away." He handed her his handkerchief to swipe away the mess.

"I noticed." Millie fastened her blouse, shifted her very wet panties back into place, and lowered her maxiskirt. She sighed. "I gotta get goin' anyway."

After a sweet kiss from Caleb, Millie headed home.

They had hidden in the shadows under the back bleachers on the football field, since no game was scheduled. Millie worked with the grounds crew and knew how to get inside.

She'd hoped being outside could help them slow down if things got too hot and heavy. *Some precaution, that was. Caleb needs to get his hands on some rubbers, or I'll wind up pregnant.* She wasn't *too* worried, though, despite their close call. Her period was due soon, and she'd pry be fine.

Actually, a bigger problem — to her way of thinking — was her *father*, who would have a cow if he knew what they had been doing. Her pa was a Baptist preacher who literally thumped the Bible. His daily admonitions were about hellfire, brimstone, repentance, and the evils of fornication. He preached his words not only from the pulpit but also from the dinner table.

She shuddered. *If I get pregnant, Pa'll take his shotgun, not to force a* weddin' *but to kill Caleb. Pa'd prefer a funeral rather than a* weddin', *and jail to marryin' me off to the likes of Caleb. The* Weather's family was Catholic. Pa didn't hold with them. No, Pa'd kill Caleb, and not likely to word no fancy-dancy ashes-to-ashes preachin' over 'im, either.

She sighed heavily. There was only one thing to do — break up with Caleb — and she better do it fast, sooner rather than later. *I have no choice. I got to put the brakes on until Pa accepts him. And truth be told, that would be never.* Was it fair to lead Caleb on when she knew she could never marry him? Could some miracle happen?

*I love Caleb with everythin' I have in me, but I've got to get real about this. A future with him isn't possible. If we continue carryin' on, somethin's bound to happen. We'll get caught — one way or another. This has to stop, not only to protect me but to also save* him. *Caleb will never understand how strong and bullheaded my pa really is. Caleb thinks our love can overcome anythin', but he's wrong. We'll never change Pa's mind.*

Millie sighed again. She really *did* love Caleb — enough to break his heart — to spare him her pa's gun. But now she had to do a complete about-face and set him free.

Plenty of girls tried flirting with Caleb, but he had made it clear he was *Millie's* beau. Maybe Amy Rae could . . . Millie was unable to complete that thought. She couldn't stand even a mental picture of anyone else in his arms.

*There's just no other way. Better he's wed to someone else than dead. How on earth can I do this? We have so much history to-gether . . .*

Millie had known Caleb forever. She'd first spied him in kindergarten and waited every day at the classroom door for him to walk in. From the get-go, all Caleb had to do was show up on the scene, and Millie would grab him by the hand and announce they were playing house. Then she'd drag him to the housekeeping corner. She was the Ma, and he was the Pa. No two ways about it. No ifs, ands, buts, or maybes either. That was the way it was. She declared it, and he'd had no rest until he complied. She *had* to play with Caleb. Period. There was nothing the teacher could do to break them apart or get them to broaden their playmates. Millie simply refused to comply.

*Pa calls me bullheaded, but I know what's what. I know what I want and when I want it, and I aim to git it, too, as surely as flies on Shinola. But I cain't git Caleb. Pa's fairly stubborn hisself.*

Caleb had always been smart, though, even in kindergar-ten. He had found a way to play house with her yet still man-aged to use toy trucks and do *menfolk things*. While Millie had pretended to cook and mother the baby dolls, he had pre-tended to hunt. He could usually be found hauling a toy truck back and forth filled with wooden animals. He'd claimed the wooden animals were meat for their supper, then he'd deepen his voice, sayin' *Girl, ah brung y'all dinner. Cook it up right quick, hear?*

She chuckled at the sweet memory. Love at first sight at age five! Caleb had always enjoyed telling folks *we fell in love in kindergarten.* And they had.

Millie had spent all her school years with Caleb. Her pa hadn't had much of a clue about them or her feelings for

Caleb. That was, until Caleb came to call on her officially to ask her to their high school sing-along.

*As soon as her pa answered the door, Caleb looked him straight in the eyes and said, "Sir, I'd like to take Millie to the Harvest Hootenanny."*

*Her pa stood ramrod straight and tall, looking grim and shaking his head no the whole while Caleb spoke.*

*Millie pleaded. "Pa, a Hootenanny is a sing-along. Ain't no sin to sing. We do it all the time at the Meetin'."*

*Pa shouted and grabbed his shotgun. "Y'all git yer sorry self out of here, boy! We don't hold with prancin' an' dancin' an' a singin' rock and roll. It's the devil's frolic."*

*Caleb took off like a shot.*

There was no way her Pa would have let her go. Not with anyone. Not even a church-going boy like Caleb. The Primitive Baptist Church her father pastored frowned on dancing and drinking and card playing. But mostly, it deplored fornicating or anything that distracted from praising God and following His laws.

Since Millie had been forbidden from going to any school dance or Hootenanny, she had found other ways of spendin' time with her beau. She felt pretty safe sneaking off with Caleb and dancing under the stars to the songs on his transistor radio. They'd danced to *Ain't No Mountain High Enough, My Cherie Amour, Can't Take My Eyes Off of You,* and even *Can't Help Falling in Love.* Sometimes they'd simply dance to the whisper of the wind in the pine treetops, but they didn't dance in public.

Her pa would kill her — literally — if he ever found out she and Caleb were together. He'd do anything to keep his kin from sin. He'd said so a million times.

After the no-go on the school songfest, they'd spent time hiking the trails in the Great Smoky Mountain National Park,

GSMNP. Occasionally, they'd lie beside the creek talking about the future and kissing — a lot of kissing. Since the woods gave them a measure of privacy, those kisses had escalated from sweet ones to French ones. Soon they couldn't keep their hands off each other and began to want *more — much more.*

It had started out innocently enough. Caleb would brush against her body by accident, or she'd accidentally touch his thigh. In time, she had sat on his lap and began kissing him while his fingers caressed her over her sweater, then things progressed.

One day, Caleb's hands, calloused by work and the fiddle he played, had slipped underneath, up, and under the confines of her bra. Delicious shivers had run through her awakening body that eventually led to deep shudders when he'd found her nipples. Warmth had pooled between her thighs. It took several weeks before his lips had followed his fingertips. He'd start out kissing her mouth, her very sensitive neck, and finally down to the crest of her breasts. Caleb's touch had been hesitant and feather-light — just what Millie had needed.

That was when Caleb had suggested one person at a time get semi-naked. Usually it was him, since he was the one with the loaded gun between his legs, and they figured he could do what he had to do — if it came to that. What that was exactly, Millie hadn't been quite sure. They had tried hard to keep her body out of the picture. Tried and failed. Again and again.

From health books and girl talk, Millie had thought she understood the term *erection*, but soon found the real deal was very different from what she'd thought. *Geesh. His thang plumps when ye cook it.*

One night, Caleb had sucked his breath in, creating enough space between his jeans and his belly.

*What's he doing?*

He took her hand to lead it past the trail of soft curling hairs until it rested *down there*, on his whatchamacallit.

Caleb's package had sprung out like a jack-in-the-box!
She giggled.

That embarrassed him, and he zipped up fast.

"Ow! Dagnabbit!" Caleb apparently caught his tender skin in his zipper.

Millie didn't giggle again, although she wanted to — it was funny. *Oops. What should I do?* Millie kissed him good night, promising herself she wouldn't laugh next time his thang went crazy. His moving part just surprised the heck out of her. Who knew man parts jumped around like that?

Millie's family lived on a small tract farm with chickens, goats, and dogs. She reckoned she knew how babies were made, but she never noticed their parts jumping. How the parts got together, she saw from farm animals. But lovemaking between a man and woman was still a mystery. *It must be a learn-by-doing kind of thing.*

Fast girls like Dede Jacobs knew about such things, but nice girls like Millie knew little. The boys seemed to flock around Dede, but Millie was happy with just Caleb. Lately, she noticed Herman Trentham making eyes at her to let her know he was interested. Still, she didn't seek out any other attention or really encourage him. Did she?

Lately, Caleb had been taking their makin'-out to whole new levels. One night, he'd asked her to *eat him,* and she'd been confused until he made it very clear that his man part was supposed to go in her *mouth!* That had been a shock, and so was the little bit of soapy tasting semen she'd gagged on. Seemed like he'd lost control darn fast. The whole thing had not held great appeal for her, but he'd been over the moon. Still, gagging wasn't any fun.

Truth be told, though, the act made her feel the power she held over Caleb. The thought was heady. Using her mouth on him had seemed to keep things in hand, manageable. At least, she knew she couldn't get pregnant *that* way.

After a while, she'd begun to feel unsatisfied with giving Caleb all the attention. New needs arose in her, heating her veins and pooling between her legs. She hadn't been sure of what to do with the new wanting and yearning growing inside of her.

Then Caleb had turned the tables and went down on *her*. Millie had thought she'd faint and was sure she died and gone straight to heaven when his tongue touched her *there*. He'd made her breathless, and she could not get over the exquisite sensations that had filled her and carried her away — way beyond even that. It beat anything she had ever known. That was when she'd first learned all about climaxing.

As time wore on, Millie had wanted more. And more. And more. Lately, the two of them had been shedding clothes like a long-haired dog every time they got together. Her body now understood the wonders of sex with Caleb like never before. She sensed the sexual pressure to take things to the next level mounting inside her. Add the overwhelming urge to merge with Caleb in every way, and it made the whole concept of giving him up for his own good far more difficult than she could imagine.

Seeing Caleb, stopping him, and parting from him was getting harder and harder. Too often, Millie found herself worrying and feeling anxious about devising reasons for not being home. *Pa cannot find out I'm seeing Caleb.* To get out of the house, she babysat for Matilde's young'uns and called Caleb to come over when she put the kids down, but it became clearer and clearer that something had to give.

*Things between us are getting too difficult to control. I have to find some way to put on the brakes, and the only way I can do that is to break up with Caleb. It will hurt my heart, but I can't do it gently. Lord, the guy would talk me out of it. He could sell sand in a sandstorm. It's so hard, especially since I don't want to break up with him. The only way to keep him safe from Pa is to find a guy from church like Herman Trentham.*

*Herman likes me. I can tell. He's been makin' eyes at me and even asked me to the Prom . . . hmm. Being the daughter of a preacher is tough.* Tears formed in Millie's eyes, but she refused to let them fall. She drew in a deep, cleansing breath to strengthen herself to do what she had to do.

Millie's mind, once made up, was something no one could change. Her will was like iron, as unbending as an oak tree. And sometimes — like now — just as nutty. For to pass on a guy like Caleb was plumb crazy. Common sense took over. She had to break up with Caleb. It was that simple, that clear, that necessary.

*I'll have to start it with Herman and end it with Caleb. Caleb will buy that I fell for another guy. After all, Caleb knows Herman is loco about me and teases me about him. Somehow, I have to let Caleb go. I love him so much, but we're as doomed as Romeo and Juliet.*

When Millie saw Caleb the next day, she acted on her plan. "This has to stop." She tried her best to keep her voice stern. "We gotta break up."

"What?" Caleb looked as shocked as if he was struck by lightning. "What the hell! You can't be serious. We've been sweet on each other since kindergarten! Break up? We love each other. Why?"

Millie swallowed, then cleared her throat. Her hand shot out to grip his arm, since he seemed poised to run and get outta Dodge or grab her right there in the hall and make a scene. She needed him to accept her hurtful words so she could keep him safe and alive. Her Pa had a temper and felt compelled by God to force his family to follow His teachings.

Caleb froze when Millie grabbed him. His fingers automatically balled into fists, itching to fight, but he held back with effort. But his body language obviously didn't stop the dreadful words pouring from Millie's mouth and not merely penetrating his heart but worse, piercing his very soul. Every word created a fresh, deep, bleeding wound, widening with each word she uttered.

Millie continued. "We're more like brother and sister, not true lovers. Surely you can see that for yourself. Admit it. We're just tinkering around, experimenting like the newspaper advice column, *Dear Abby*, says. If this was true love, we'd be like elk in rutting season. We don't cut it."

He turned and stared straight into her eyes, trying to read her mind. "Is that what you think last night—and all the other nights—were? Brother and sister? I'm right sure they don't do what we did."

Millie shifted her weight and shook her head with sadness. "Didn't you notice we never do more than pet? One of us always stops. True love doesn't weigh the consequences like we do. If we were truly in love, nothing could stop us. But we . . . we stop on a dime. I want the whole kettle of fish. That *zing* the songs and books talk about."

"That's fiction. Ain't real. More than what? Sex? Of course, I noticed that we always stop. That's the failsafe *plan*. We make a point to stop before things go too far. I thought we agreed on that—waiting until we were married to *go all the way*. Hell, I was *saving* myself for marriage. *Our* marriage. I thought you were, too."

Silently she nodded. " I know, we said that . . . but—"

"Sister, eh? Ha!" His self-control slipped into full-on anger. "I thought you felt the same way. You sure had me fooled." He held his stance rigid. It took all he had not to break down and blubber like a little girl. Thank God the tardy bell would sound any second.

"Caleb, we just don't have *enough* chemistry . . ." Mille murmured.

He stood openmouthed, unable to form a response. He forced words past his strangled throat. "Chemistry is a class I take—not a feeling, not something we haven't got."

Millie lifted her chin. "There's not enough fireworks going off when we touch. I want that *zing* folk talk about, I tell you. What we have can't penetrate your Catholic guilt either." She sighed. "It ain't enough. We need chemistry."

He stood stock-still, and a quip slipped out before he could stop it. "Chemistry's not what you signed up for. You're enrolled in English. Chemistry isn't your bag, remember?"

Millie blew her bangs upward with a forceful breath. "That was lame. Don't be cute. This is serious and no joking matter."

"So, shoot me for being a gentleman and respecting you." He couldn't keep iciness from his voice. "What the hell? What's religion got to do with it? I'm not that religious, and I know for a fact you aren't either. Your church doesn't even permit dancing." He paused and studied her for a moment. "That's why we're not going to Prom. At least, that's what you said."

Millie's face flushed. It was a dead giveaway that worried Caleb. He'd caught her regretful tone as she spoke, which only served to confuse him more.

"About the Prom." Millie paused with a sigh. "Better get everything on the table, since it's happening in early May this year. Herman Trentham did ask me, and . . . uh . . . yes, I said I'd break the rules and go with him. We're gonna sneak out . . ."

Caleb felt the shock hit his system with more than the *zing* she was talking about. Talk about a punch to the gut. *Hell, we have plenty of zing. I almost went inside her all the way instead of just using the tip of my cock* . . . His heart shattered. He looked down at the ground, surprised shards of his heart weren't scattered there willy-nilly.

The second last-call bell rang. They headed down the hallway toward their classes. He couldn't help but ask, "What about the two-point-five kids we were gonna have? I have plenty of zing . . . What the hell's Catholic guilt anyway?"

Millie sighed again, and a testy tone replaced her softer, regretful one. "That doesn't matter."

Anger laced his tone. "It mattered enough to bring it up, so it does matter. To me at least."

"Catholics feel guilty about having sex before marriage." She shrugged. "I don't see myself marrying you. That was a dream we had. Puppy love . . . I love you, of course I do, but I'm not *in love* with you. Does that make sense?"

His shoulders tensed. "No. About as much sense as non-sense makes. If you'll pardon me, I have a *chemistry* class to attend. And I'm clearly tardy." Still, he lingered at the door of the Chem Lab, steeling himself, hoping the lab work would get his mind off her shocking words. *In love . . . Love . . . What the hell is the difference?*

"Caleb . . ." Millie began, then stopped.

He started to turn away but paused.

"We can talk on the bus ride home," Millie murmured. "About the Prom and all . . ."

"No need. I have Debate Club today. Not riding the bus. I have nothing left to say. I love you, Millie. I thought we were getting hitched after graduation like we'd talked about. But don't worry about me none." His shoulders slumped as he turned to enter his class. He didn't watch her go, but he thought he heard a faint sniffle echo in the hall.

That was the day something in Caleb died. Not long after that, Caleb heard rumors that Millie had been seen hanging out regularly with Herman. And to top it all off, he learned she sure as hell did plan to go to Prom despite her father. How she was gonna pull that off was none of his beeswax.

# CHAPTER TWO: YOUNG LOVE

April 1969

Caleb tried to act friendly with Millie whenever their paths crossed, but he just couldn't manage that. It was simply too hard. Friendship with her didn't cut it. His love was definitely not puppy love, no matter what Millie said. Millie could think what she wanted, but he knew first cuts ran deepest, and this was one of those. *First cut? Last cut is what I think. I'm never gonna fall for that crap again.*

He tried not to care what Millie thought. He was too sad to be mad or vengeful, but secretly he was very deeply shaken. His world had turned upside down. He'd lost his anchor and drifted in a world of pain and longing. He decided to close and lock the door to his heart.

"Time moves on and heals all wounds." His Aunt Emma Jean — or Auntie Em, as he'd called her since he was a tyke — had told him that when his folks died and many times afterward.

He sure hoped her words were true, but he didn't feel his broken heart would ever heal. Instead, he tried to turn his attention elsewhere, to other things that were happening around him.

Hippies and the peace movement had burst on the scene seemingly overnight — like everything else in his life. One day, he had two loving parents, the next, he had none. One day he had Millie, the next, he lost her. One day his hair was short, and the next, he began to grow it out. The only constant in life had become change.

The hippies talked about free love. Forget the rules. Forget the confines of marriage. *Well, I, for one, am turned on with that one. What good did fidelity and celibacy do me? Millie is probably fucking Herman's brains out. I'm done with all that bullshit.*

As time moved on, Caleb noted Auntie Em's compressed lips, ignored Uncle Jacob's words about his lengthening locks, and kept his own counsel. His aunt seemed to understand his change. She knew he was hurting, everyone did, but she made sure to point out that other trout swam in the rocky stream.

Caleb never tried to woo Millie back—he never got the chance. Even as a child, she ran the ship. The proverb said *you can lead the horse to water* . . . His update on the old adage? He was certain he couldn't get that dang horse to float on its back! *Not me, at least. Maybe Herman can.*

As always, he turned to his fiddle. He had become well-known for his ability to out-fiddle just about anyone. Many veteran fiddlers had put him to the challenge. As a result, he'd began to experiment with different ways to hold it. He got more proficient when he held his fiddle in the middle of his chest, forgoing the traditional way to play.

He planned to fiddle up a storm at Prom. Millie had enjoyed his fiddlin' until she dumped him. No matter how he tried, his unhappiness at her actions still bled through his music. No more *Turkey in the Straw*, for now anyway. More like *Danny Boy*. He was way too upset for happy music.

The fiddle gave voice to his pain. He'd fiddle away any time he needed to let his agony loose.

His ma, Hettie Weathers, had killed his first tick when he was a toddler. Using a master fiddler's bow for the deed guaranteed he, too, would become a music man. Setting up lessons with his Uncle Lem was one of the last things his ma had done before her untimely death. His Auntie Em had made sure Caleb had continued those lessons.

As Caleb grew, he had taught himself to play the harmonica, finding it easier to carry with him on his treks through the forest whenever he sought tranquility. He found peace in the cathedral of green where the trees talked to his soul, healing him. He sought out their serenity every chance he got. He'd sit for hours, playing either his fiddle or his harmonica, and added his voice to convey his feeling through his tunes to the whispering pines. The hardwood's knocks, creaks, and groans were pleasant accompaniments.

Caleb spent weeks licking his wounds, then — finally — shook off a measure of pain. He stiffened his spine and carried on. Reeling with the quick turn his life took, he decided to use the money he'd been saving for a diamond engagement ring to make a down payment on a used red Ford pickup truck. *I aim to fuckin' start over. I don't need no woman to make me whole, not when I got these hills to hunt and climb. Hmm . . . Can't hunt in the Park unless there's a boar cull sanctioned by the National Park Service.* The boar was not native to the Park, and the NPS only sanctioned hunts periodically.

Caleb also started looking for a hunting dog as much as for the companionship as for the hunt. *I'll find me a good huntin' dog and then join the next boar hunt. Meanwhile, I need to help Auntie Em and Uncle Jacob run the Lodge, because John sure the hell isn't. He's chasing his dreams and racing off to college with his girl. Besides, Auntie Em has enough to worry about, what with Uncle Jacob getting older. I can't just take off and leave them high and dry. It's the least I can do for Auntie Em and Uncle Jake.*

Caleb's cousin John was more a brother cuz they were raised side by side since Caleb's parents' deaths. While John was off doing his thing, Caleb was stuck at home. Even though they both espoused and yearned to be part of the counterculture, they remained committed to the nation and had discussed the dreaded draft constantly.

While John struggled with his love of country and his desire for his love, Marsha, Caleb was no longer sure about any of it anymore. *Love? Ha! Free love? Why the hell not? I'm done with that marriage shit. I'm not gonna be a man-whore, but neither is Catholic guilt gonna crush me. I lost Millie over sex — which sucks. Not gonna happen twice. I'll be responsible and go to Confession when I need to, but that's it for celibacy. Too bad I'm not seeing anyone special.*

# CHAPTER THREE: DO YOU WANT TO KNOW A SECRET?

May 1969

M illie could see the pain in Caleb's eyes, and it killed her to know it was because of what she'd done. But with all she had on her plate now, she just couldn't worry about it. Any second now, her period should begin—shouldn't it? *Wait, no — eek — it's overdue! I'm never late, let alone overdue.*

Despite how often she checked her panties for the minutest droplet of red or brown, there wasn't a speck. She had to face it. She officially skipped her period! She couldn't imagine how she could be pregnant based on how religious she and Caleb were to prevent it. She was as regular as a Swiss clock. She and Herman hadn't even . . .

Then the truth of it slapped her in the face. *Somehow, some way, some semen — Caleb's semen — got close enough to my very wet vagina and swam upstream. Holy shit, I'm a pregnant virgin! I can't marry Caleb. Pa would kill him on sight. My path outta this mess is to marry Herman — fast.* She could hardly believe she was pregnant, but she knew if she married Herman pronto, he'd think she'd conceived on their wedding night.

Millie was determined to become Herman's wife. As far as her pa was concerned, he too would figure she got pregnant on their wedding night. She knew Herman would believe she did, provided her developing plan worked. There was one last thing she had to do for Caleb first.

Once she got home from work, she went to the kennel. Pa

had built it for the hounds he bred and currently stood inside working with the dogs. She took the wee pup from Sadie, their best coonhound breeder of hunting dogs. The puppies were weaned and ready for new owners. Millie cuddled the smallest of the litter into her warmth.

Her pa frowned at her. "Why do you bother with that runt? Ah told ya, I'ma fixin' on one for Herman."

"I want it."

Pa's tone turned stern. "You cain't keep that puny thing."

"A friend of mine," Millie continued, "sorely needs a pet." She could be as stubborn as her pa, given the circumstances. She *needed* that dog bad, and she aimed to get it. She gave him her sweetest smile. "Please, Pa, with sugar on top."

Pa grunted in response and thrust out his chin, then shrugged. "Ain't worth nuthin'. Fine. G'wan. Hope yer friend don't want much, cuz she shore ain't worth her feed."

Millie knew Caleb was usually in town on Mondays, so she set out for the Lodge, hoping Caleb's aunt would welcome the puppy. She wrapped the pup in a piece of the old blanket with her litter scent on it, then made the trip to the Lodge.

She placed the dog in Emma Jean's arms. "Caleb needs something to comfort him."

Emma Jean answered simply. "He needs *you*. But a dog *from* you might ease his pain some. Get him hunting and maybe living again. I bear you no ill will. You're young and have your reasons. Lord only knows what they are. No matter, I gotta admit, your pa'd never let the two of you wed. So sure, I'll take the puppy. You're still welcome here—just so you know."


Caleb was in a foul mood when he got home. The topic his buddies debated was over the war in Viet Nam. His forehead crunched with the dark path his mind took but lightened when he saw his aunt bearing a tiny bit of a puppy with the most striking coloring he had ever seen. Her big amber eyes glowed in her little face, and he felt a smile tug at his lips.

"Whatcha got there, Auntie Em?"

She returned his smile as the puppy raised its head, giving her a wet kiss. "Someone I know needs some love."

He shrugged. "Don't you worry none about me."

A wide grin stretched across Auntie Em's face. She winked at him and then looked down to her arms. "I was talking about this pup."

He shuffled sheepishly. "She is mighty cute. Is that a Maples' hound?"

Auntie Em nodded. "She's sweet as a sweet potato pie. Hasn't moved a muscle since she got here 'cept to give me that slobbery kiss."

"Whatcha gonna name her?" he asked.

"Ain't mine to name. She's yourn." Auntie Em sometimes lapsed heavily into her Smoky Mountain dialect, hence words like *ain't, hain't, cain't,* and *yourn* peppered her speech every now again.

Truth be told, everyone Caleb knew lapsed into it eventually. The original settlers of the area were of Scott-Irish blood, and traces of Middle Age English dialect littered their speech.

He stared at his aunt in surprise, his mouth gaping as it dawned on him. "Mine?"

"Time you get yerself a dog."

Caleb grinned. "She ain't bigger than a Tater Tot."

The name stuck. *Tater* it was.

Turned out Tater was the perfect dog for him. While the breed was often stubborn, they were also known to love their owners. And Auntie Em didn't mind having her underfoot and shook her head laughing when the zany pup found one of Caleb's socks to play with. Tater would hold it in her mouth, her head cocked as if she were saying, *Look what I got* as she waited for Caleb to chase her for it. At first, he did, and that was when it became a game.

A vigorous tug of war usually followed a chase, then Tater would tucker out, plop down, and promptly fall asleep at Caleb's knees. When he ignored the sock, Tater'd whine and cock her head as if to say, *Yoo-hoo. Look what I got. Don't you want it back?* The pup, dangling the dark sock from her mouth, looked like a Snoopy dog cartoon with a droopy black mustache. Except wherever Snoopy was white, Tater was either brown or black.

Caleb had planned to name a dog—a male coon dog he hadn't got around to getting—Phoenix. He'd reckoned to rise again himself as the name promised. But this dog followed him everywhere, and her puppy antics lifted his heart. His dog was so darn cute he called her Cutie when no one else was around.

He almost laughed when his Uncle Jacob asked, "What kinda name is Tater for a huntin' dog?"

Caleb's reply was simple. "She's small as a tater and as sweet as a tater pie."

Jacob guffawed. "That there pup is too sweet. My bet is she won't hunt." Suddenly, Tater ran off and started barking up a storm. They set off chasing her and found her staring down a very startled bear. Amazingly, the *bear* was the one who took off running. "Ah'll be durned. That pup has gumption, after all. Looks like Ah gotta eat me words. Not sure how smart that is, though."

The next time Tater took off with his sock, Caleb shook his head. "Shoulda named ye Socks."

Tater cocked her head and yipped.

Her oversized paws often tripped her when she tried to run, but she was the sweetest thing Caleb had ever seen. Tater learned fast and trained easily, but he enjoyed the fact she looked at him with adoring eyes and stuck to his side like *Velcro*, unlike the gal who walked away.

Caleb often got woke up in front of the fireplace with Tater curled on his chest. His Auntie Em would shake him and laugh as she claimed he and Tater were snoring in unison. Other times, Caleb lazed around with one sock on while the other sock was in Tater's mouth. If Tater needed to go out, she'd lick his bare foot, which got him up fast. What cracked him up the most was when Tater picked up a devotional with a picture of Jesus on the cover.

Auntie Em chuckled. "Looks like yer girl jist found Jesus."

Caleb smiled and declared Tater was one smart pooch despite what Uncle Jake claimed.

# CHAPTER FOUR: DREAMIN' AND SCHE-MIN'

Mid-May 1969

Millie thought fast, deciding on employing a plan used from the beginning of time. She took a deep breath and plunged ahead. First, seduce, second, marry Herman quick — a simple move from first base to home base in one night. Third, a conversation with Pa. *I'm a good catch, and so is Herman. Pa'd go for it. Prom Night will be much more than a big dance for sure.*

After Prom night, she knew Herman would stake his claim. *He* was her man and would plan to be forevermore, she was certain. She didn't know much, but she knew a faithful church goin' Baptist boy like Herman would not just casually mess with the pastor's daughter and skip out on her.

Preparing for the big night made her as jumpy as a squirrel surprised by a barking dog who'd found a coon, but she could do it. She had to.

The Prom itself was a blur. When she saw Caleb had Amy Rae on his arm, she sighed and pasted a smile on her face. She was a tad irritated when Caleb picked up his fiddle and began playing. Nobody could resist his music, and she was no exception.

Caleb was in prime form. Everyone gathered 'round and forgot about dancing once he got up to speed. He was that good. After a time, Caleb removed his suit jacket and played with more enthusiasm until the bowstrings snapped. When Caleb rolled his shirtsleeves up his arm, Millie sighed as she recalled running her fingers through the dark hairs of his well-formed muscles. She shook herself free of those thoughts. *Stop. Focus on tonight, not Caleb.*

Once Caleb stepped down from the stage, Millie turned her full attention back to her plans for Prom *night*. She'd worn her hair down, and her Prom dress was a lovely concoction of ivory chiffon cascading from her slightly widening—not yet noticeable—pregnancy. She set her mind to seducing Herman.

She managed to lure Herman into an empty classroom. A tender kiss and a simple touch, and the encounter turned extremely passionate. Millie smiled and congratulated herself. *Step one done. Now for the rest.*

Herman was tender and treated her with love and devotion and seemed to know what he was doing once they got going. There was no fumbling. The full-skirted Prom dress made things easy.

After they were done, Herman gaped, looking shocked. "Oh geezmateez. Uh, I didn't mean to . . . Marry me, okay? All we did was get a jump on our wedding night. I was gonna propose Graduation Day. I want to be with you for the rest of my life. I hope you'll do me the honor."

"I will." She gave him a sweet smile and a quick kiss to seal the deal.

The next morning, Millie approached her pa as soon as he had his coffee. "Pa, I need marryin', or I'm gonna become a fallen woman. Herman wants to marry me, and I don't think I can hold myself or him back anymore."

While things happened as fast as a shotgun wedding, no gun was involved. Without a doubt, there would have been, had the groom been Caleb—assuming Caleb survived the proposal announcement.

Pa married Herman and Millie the following Saturday afternoon. Pa asked no questions. Millie wore her ivory Prom dress for the ceremony, but her ma, June, added a quickly made fingertip-veil to the ensemble.

Her ma gave her a small smile. "Ah told ye from the git-go, this dress was made for a weddin'."

With considerable effort, Millie shoved Caleb out of her mind and concentrated on her new life as Herman's bride.

The whole town had expected Millie to choose Caleb, but sadly, that was not to be. Her friends were somewhat surprised that she had thrown Caleb aside and then up and married Herman, but they weren't bothered by the suddenness of the entire thing. It just made Caleb more eligible to others. Folks 'round town felt when something ended abruptly, God had a better plan in mind.

Millie's friends often commented on how smitten she appeared, and she did nothing to correct their perception. She adored Herman. His only fault was not being Caleb.

*Chimney-corner law* of the south went into effect, and from then on, no one ever talked about Caleb and Millie as a couple again. Not in public nor in private. Granny women could, but no one else.

Seemed almost the instant the Prom was over, Caleb had become *the* most popular bachelor in town. Graduation was over and done, and he was now regarded as a man of marryin' age. In this new age of free love, women had started asking *him* out, and he accepted even though his heart was not in it. He quickly learned to chat up women without becoming emotionally attached. Not wanting to be a heartbreaker, he always made it clear he wasn't interested in anything permanent relationship-wise. Of course, he didn't turn down what most of the ladies offered freely and took to carrying condoms with him everywhere. *Hmph . . . So much for Catholic guilt.*

Caleb became much sought after by the single gals at St. Mary's Catholic Church and other ladies in the area. Soon he became the target for the granny women of the town and surrounding hamlets. They set him up on many blind dates with marriage in mind. He knew their schemin' but wasn't fallin' for it.

His first Annual Chicken Dinner Auction held at St. Mary's was fun, but no woman captured his interest, let alone his heart. Not even the chestnut-haired Amy Rae. He'd told her at the Prom he wasn't planning on marrying any time soon. She never pressured him and always said *yes* to dates whenever he asked. In turn, he didn't pressure her for sex either. That did not extend to Dede Jacobs, however. That girl was very much into *free lovin'*.

With all the dating he did, he led no one on. He had still to get over Millie. It was truly a new world out there for him—one he could barely keep up with. He kept busy at the Lodge, helping his Auntie Em while his cousin John was off working on his degree in Kentucky at Berea College.

# CHAPTER FIVE: A CHANGE IS GONNA COME

August 1969

Caleb identified with the folk song saying times were a-changin'. *Didn't Dylan sing that? Or maybe the Byrds? Who cared? Someone sang it. Could be Peter, Paul, and Mary, for all I know.* He cringed at even the sound of the word *marry*. It always brought Millie to mind, and not in a good way. *I sure do hate running into Millie and Herman. They look like they've never been happier. Gotta get on with my life. Breaking up with Millie was sure hard, and reclaiming my heart is nearly impossible, but I aim to do it even if it kills me.*

Change was happening in the world, and Caleb did his best to welcome it. Others his age were setting their sights on new and different priorities. A new consciousness swept across the country, and the counterculture sprung up as a result. Things sometimes felt upside down. Nothing was the same, but he managed to go with the flow.

The next day was an ordinary day at the Lodge with Caleb helping Jacob and Emma Jean run things. The weather was no better and no worse than usual. Everything was average with no more or less guests, no more or less diners, no more or less walk-ins, and no more or less staff. Suddenly, out of the blue, Jacob made a loud snorting, snoring sound and collapsed behind the Lodge registration counter. There was no time to do anything and no one to call.

Emma Jean ran to Jacob's side. Caleb had to move and

move fast. Jacob was unconscious.

They shook him and finally roused him. Somehow between them, Emma Jean and Caleb got Jacob in the truck and headed for Mountain Heritage Hospital. All Caleb could see was a blur of activity at the hospital until Emma Jean sent him off to notify John, who was away in college. In Kentucky!

Emma Jean insisted Caleb drive to get John while she tried to deal with Jacob. John needed to be notified of Jacob's apparent heart attack.

The next thing he knew, he was in Uncle Jacob's pickup headed for John. *Shhhiiit on a stick. I never been out of Knoxville or even on the Interstate 75, or I-75 as folks call it.* He stopped at any rest stops he could find to ask directions. He needn't have worried. There were plenty of signs advertising mountain-made arts and crafts that the Berea students made and sold.

Once he arrived on campus, he was overwhelmed. He had never seen so many buildings nor such beautiful, well-tended grounds. He drove around the college but had no luck finding his cousin at all. It had been easier to find Berea College than to locate John. There was no sign of him anywhere. He couldn't track down Marsha, either. *If time is a gift like Auntie Em claims, I want to return today and yesterday, too.*

He finally found the Admissions Office, and they told him where John's dorm was. Come to find out, many had students left campus for the mother of all concerts, a three-day festival of peace, love, and music called Woodstock. In New York.

*Shit, I'd have liked to go, too. The closest thing I have to show is a plastic set of purple love beads.* He shook his head. *This line of thinkin' ain't bringing me any closer to findin' John.*

After convincing the resident assistant, RA, he was John Weather's relative there on a family emergency, he managed to get John's class schedule. He looked in several buildings but failed to find him—even going as far as Boone Hotel and Restaurant where John worked. Frustrated and having no other option, he talked the RA into letting him bunk in John's room.

On Tuesday, two full days later, Caleb finally found his cousin.

John was spaced out, hungover, smelling like a hog, and *married* to boot. Caleb pushed John, clothes and all, into an icy shower. Then he handed him a razor to shave. When John grabbed a Woodstock t-shirt saying *Peace*, Caleb threw him a clean shirt that sported the Berea College logo.

John caught it and complained, "Dude, I'm still wet."

"You bet your ass you're *all wet*. Shake it off. Man up. Your pa's in the hospital." Caleb was pissed about John's *Peace* t-shirt.

John went from dazed to crazed and hurried to get with it. He hopped around on one foot, trying to dress and get his shoe on at the same time.

*I'll give him peace all right. A piece of my mind.* Then Caleb *made* John drink a gallon of strong black coffee. He hustled John's sorry ass into the truck to head back to Tennessee. They didn't have time for him farting around like this. Two days lost looking for him.

Caleb could barely stand to talk to John. He'd been off having a good time—at Woodstock no less—while his pa was at Mountain Heritage Hospital, leaving Caleb to carry the burden of family obligations. Caleb took his duty seriously and hated to fail the family.

The whole ride home, all John did was yammer about Marsha. *She didn't know where he was. She'd be mad he was gone. She wouldn't even know why.* On and on.

Caleb's patience was wearing thin. *Maybe John's in shock or in denial. Maybe he's worried sick and distracting himself.* Caleb wished he could be distracted, too, but the stakes were too high.

Unfortunately, when they reached the hospital, they

learned later that Jacob had had a doozy of a heart attack. Both he and John were needed to pick up the slack and help Auntie Em run the Lodge as she cared for Uncle Jacob.

John never made it back to complete his degree. Running the Lodge had become their life until that fateful day when the National Draft Lottery took place.

Caleb wouldn't ever forget that infamous day crowded around the television when the Draft Lottery announcement came on. John's number was up. He'd won the lottery that no one ever wanted to win.

Caleb's number hadn't been called, but he had an obligation, too. He had to step up to family duty. The times called them both to service, ending their dreams of flower power, hippies, and free love. While once only teetering on the threshold of manhood, Caleb had to man up and take charge.

# CHAPTER SIX: WALK ON BY

1970

It took some talking for Millie to convince Miss Emma Jean to allow her to work even part-time at the Lodge again. But Emma Jean was known to have a soft heart. Millie needed both the work and the money. Since Millie had a flair for cooking, Emma Jean began to teach her all she knew. She specialized in grits, greens, and pork and taught Millie how to cook good old country comfort food.

Emma Jean also kept Millie out of Caleb's sight as much as she could.

Millie appreciated that, because every time she caught sight of him, her blood ran hot, and she remembered being in his arms, kissing him, loving him. Unfortunately, she even remembered his dripping cock.

Despite her feelings, Millie attempted to follow the path the songs outlined on the radio—lyrics that pleaded with an old lover to just walk on by and pay her no mind. However, no matter how much she tried, she *still* noticed Caleb's tears. His sadness. And remembered his pain when she'd said goodbye. She prayed her gift of the puppy had given Caleb the love she had denied him.

Millie had lied to Caleb about *Puppy Love* being all they had between them. Adults labeled first love as puppy love that didn't count for much in the grand scheme. However, what she and Caleb shared had been serious—very serious—and she knew that. It had been a Herculean task to convince Caleb that theirs wasn't *true* love. She hadn't needed to say more, since her actions had done what her words could not. Her marriage had been a clear message.

Still, Millie ached. To see Caleb that unhappy made her feel just awful about breaking his heart. She missed him and tried never to compare Herman to him. Whenever she ran into him, she felt the blood drain from her face. The feelings intensified when he took pains to steer clear of her. Despite her actions, the rebuff killed her and shook her to her core. *If I weren't pregnant . . . Stop it. You could never have Caleb. You know Pa'd have more than a simple conniption. He'd have killed Caleb, and you darn well know that.*

She redoubled her attempts to make Herman her man in every way possible, doing her level best to avoid Caleb.

Mille adjusted to married life more easily than to her blossoming abdomen. *I hope I don't get too big too fast. So far, my baby is a teeny tiny blip on my body. All too soon, I'll really show.* She was pleased her plan to both seduce and marry Herman had worked. But she wasn't thrilled that she had done it the way she had to do it. She'd had no real choice in the matter. It was either seduce Herman and marry Herman, or else. That way, she could have this baby without endangering Caleb.

In the past, Caleb's magic fingers had managed to break her maiden tissue during their make-out sessions. Herman hadn't seemed to notice much less care. He had just focused on her and the joy of their union. What would have happened to her and the baby had Herman not married her? Would she have to seek out a witch to brew her some concoction to cause her to miscarry? She couldn't bear that thought. Thankfully, Herman had no clue the baby wasn't his and no cause to think otherwise. Why would he?

She was frankly relieved that she was married. She could no more give up this baby than she could give up breathing. Feeling bad about her baby wasn't possible. Not marrying Caleb, on the other hand, was something altogether different.

Still, though, she did have trouble herself *believing* she was pregnant. *Who gets pregnant like that?* She and Caleb had worked *their* brand of birth control so religiously, yet a baby was on the way. The conception had happened so miraculously she wondered *what* the Almighty had planned for this baby to do in life. Cure cancer? Miss Emma Jean often said, *Man plans, God laughs*, so He must be laughing up a storm at this turn of events.

Too often, fatigue washed over her like a tidal wave and had her napping for the first time since she was in diapers. Usually, naps left her nauseous and feeling groggy and sluggish. Not so anymore, thank heaven. At first, she continued working at the Lodge and had no problems. But after a while, she could barely hold it together. She grew too exhausted to work the lunch bunch crowd. Instead, she would return to the cabin she shared with Herman and sleep. Growing a baby was exhausting. *Who knew?*

Lately, however, when she awoke from her afternoon nap, nausea began in earnest. Followed not long after with full-on vomiting. Whatever she managed to eat came right back up. *At least morning sickness is keeping my weight down. Sometimes, I swear my midwife knows I'm farther along than I admit, but the woman never breathed a word about it. She merely said . . .* First babies are born whenever. Early, late, who knows? *I wonder if my baby will look like me or . . .* Her breath stopped. *I pray to God this baby looks like me.*

Millie found it painful and unnatural to see Caleb and not fess up. Not tell him she still loved him. Not tell him she always would. Not tell him this baby was his.

While it was too late for her and Caleb, she and Herman became parents of twin baby girls that winter. It seemed like the first time she and Herman made love after their births, she conceived again.

1972

One afternoon in the spring, Millie, noticeably pregnant again, ran into Caleb at the Battles Grocery Store. She couldn't quite catch her breath when she saw the tall hunk he had become. Her heart pounded in her chest, and she was surprised to feel her body shake with long-suppressed yearning. She prayed her emotional condition wasn't as obvious as her pregnancy.

Millie had her two chubby little girls inside the shopping cart. They both wore baby-face smiles covered in cookie crumbs. One little one stretched out a sticky hand to offer Caleb a much-gummed cookie. He smiled and looked at the girls. Then he took a second look.

*Was there a glint in his eye? Or a squint? Did he suspect anything?*

Millie had to admit her girls were darling. She flushed and introduced them. "This 'uns Emmie Jo and, this un's Joy June." Her hand strayed to her belly, "Don't know what the new one will be. Too bad we don't have a crystal ball to tell us iffen it's a boy or a girl."

"Please to meetcha, little missies. Darn but they look—"

Millie was quick to jump in, saying, "Like me and my ma, I know. Herman says so every day. Talk about family resemblance." She held her breath, hoping he'd gloss over the girls' names.

He frowned as he scratched his head. "Riiight, your *ma* . . . weren't those the names we picked out?" His tone could cut glass.

Millie spoke in a rush. "They're such pretty names. They shouldn't go to waste. Your aunt has been so good to me, and Joy June is named for Ma. I'm sorry if that was thoughtless of me."

"Looks like you're getting your fondest wish, a passel of young'uns."

Millie shifted uncomfortably. "No, that was *you* who was

after a bunch of munchkins." She flushed, then laughed as she brushed the hair out of her eyes with a shaky hand. She looked down at her swollen womb and shook her head. "Not that it matters none."

Caleb repeatedly shuffled his feet, re-balancing his stance and shifting his weight, clearly uncomfortable with their encounter and conversation.

Millie made hesitant moves to leave, focusing on her fussing kidlets. *Is he suspicious? How could he be? I can hardly believe I have kids myself — twins in particular. Is his discomfort because of me? In spite of me? The kids? The past?* She sighed heavily.

There it was again. That sad look in Caleb's eyes, which made her heart hurt.

Millie ignored it and moved forward. "Gotta git goin' while these two are still behaving. Don't want no fuss. Iffen I don't get a move on, they'll miss their naps, and I'll have hell on steroids dealing with them. Nuthin' worse than overtired young'uns."

Caleb seemed to shake off whatever bothered him. It was increasingly apparent he was preparing to skedaddle, too. "Nice seeing you again and . . . your kids." He looked like he'd have tipped his hat had he been wearing one. In any case, he sure showed he'd had enough by leaving.

Millie's young'uns demanding attention meant she needed to focus, but she just couldn't. In a hurry now, she didn't consult her shopping list. Instead, she threw random items into her cart, a clear sign she was more shaken by the encounter with Caleb than she wanted to be. In a rush, she headed to the cashier. *Gotta get out of here before I break down.* She spotted a full and abandoned shopping cart in the aisle and wondered if it was Caleb's. If so, he must be upset, too.

When she got home, she put the children down for their naps. She donned her apron and began unpacking the groceries, only to discover she had bought enough pickles to feed Sevier County!

Millie's shaky hand moved over her pounding heart, rubbing it to slow it down. *Phew, that was a close call. I hope Caleb never figures it out. It was bad enough dealing with Miss Emma Jean.* She recalled an incident shortly after Emma Jean had allowed her to become part-time help in the kitchen. When Emma Jean had seen the girls for the first time, the twins had just started walking. Like Caleb, Emma Jean had also taken a second look.

*When they were peeling carrots for a beef stew, Emma Jean said, "They look like Caleb did when he was their age."*

*Surprised, Millie nicked herself and dropped the vegetable peeler. She sucked on the finger to stop the small cut from bleeding.*

*In a quiet voice, Emma Jean spoke again. "I'm no one to judge, and I'm not judging you. Not many know this, but Caleb's ma was a redhead. Ever notice his hair looks copper when the sun hits it just right?" She paused and took the freshly peeled carrots, slicing them into quarter-sized chunks. "Does he know? Will you ever tell him?"*

*With a quiet shake of her head, Millie murmured, "I don't rightly know." She wondered if Caleb suspected what Emma Jean did.*

*Emma Jean simply nodded and said, "Some things are better left unspoken, Millie. If ever a time comes to say something, you'll know. We don't need to discuss it. I have eyes and can see for myself what's what. No need to bother Caleb with it."*

After that encounter at the market, sweet memories of dancing with Caleb to the music on transistor radio overwhelmed Millie. The thought of those under-the-stars dances and fervent kisses made her realize just how much she had given up. Herman had never had the time to court her. *Must be karma. I'm getting what I gave. I love Herman. I went after him, and he's given me no complaints. No man could have treated me any better or loved me more than Herman does. Seeing Caleb again stirred up feelings I didn't expect, is all. Must be my hormones acting up.*

Nonetheless, tears gathered in her eyes and threatened to fall down her face. With an effort, she tried to pull herself together. When she felt strong arms enfold her, she leaned back against Herman's solid frame letting her tears stream from her eyes.

He turned her to face him and said, "Hey, hey, what's all this about? What's wrong?"

She picked a corner of her apron and dabbed at her eyes. "I'm just feelin' like the luckiest gal in Sevier County. Makes me choke up. Countin' my blessings with y'all. Moved me to these silly tears. The having a baby thingy, I reckon."

"I'm the lucky one," he said. "Why don't you lie down? I'll slap some burgers on the grill for supper. Give those dogs a rest now, hear?" He gently steered her to the living room couch. As he went about gathering the food item, he said, "I'll get some hot dogs out for the twins."

She complied. "You're a good man, Herman."

"Her man? Say what? You got that wrong, Mrs. Trentham. I'm *your* man, not her man."

Millie chuckled at his lame but frequent joke. She didn't deserve him. And she sure as hell didn't deserve Caleb either.


After seeing Millie at the grocer's, Caleb began hiking in earnest to cope with his unsettled feelings. Any time he could, he'd escaped into the calming folds of the Smoky Mountains, exploring its trails, rocks, and rills. He often played his harmonica. Sometimes his tunes were mournful and prolonged, expressing his longing for a life he wanted but could not have. Other times, he was rejuvenated and played joyful jigs as he sat a while watching the butterflies play, the fish jump, and the birds fly from branch to branch. Occasionally their trilling seemed to accompany his melodies.

Over time, he managed to climb all five trails to the summit of Mount LeConte. His favorite was the Alum Cave Trail, which eventually led him to the LeConte Lodge. He was up there so many times, he got to know the staff and met Hikin' Hugh Robertson, a former senior ranger familiar with the backcountry trails. Hugh introduced him to Jack Huff, one of the original founders. Paul Adams had first established Camp LeConte, which soon became known as the primitive and rustic LeConte Lodge. Jack Huff and his wife had taken over and had been managing LeConte Lodge ever since.

1973

Caleb could not believe how fast time flew. On an unseasonably warm March day, seeking peace and quiet, he decided to go fishing. He headed to Little Pigeon River off the *Spur*, a small portion of US 441 between Pigeon Forge and Gatlinburg. The passage of time became apparent when he saw Millie again.

Millie and her children were wading in the shallow water, picking up stones and river rocks, giggling and screeching. Millie's strawberry blonde hair shone in the bright sunlight. Gone was her girlish figure, and gone was his heart all over again.

Millie's two little redheaded girls were splashing each other, and a little boy held her hand as he gingerly stepped into the lazy current. Her figure was full, and Caleb wondered if she was pregnant again. He shook his head and grimaced, moving upstream and around the bend, hoping to avoid them. But they, too, must have moved because he almost caught a kid with his last cast.

Millie raised a hand to shield her eyes from the streaming sunlight. She called out to her flock when she saw they were perilously close to an angler. She squinted toward him and stopped suddenly.

Caleb figured from her frozen stance she must have recognized him. He froze, too, but he couldn't help checking her out. The girl of his teens had become one hundred percent woman, and it looked dang good on her. Seeing her with her kids hurt as if he had been shot straight through the heart. He had grown a beard, so maybe that accounted for the hesitancy he noticed. He gulped. He had known Millie had had children, but he wasn't prepared to meet any more of 'em. Yet despite its flood of tourists, they lived in a small town, so avoiding each other altogether wasn't quite possible . . . obviously.

As Millie got closer, she quickly introduced him to her little'uns. "This is Mama's friend from school, Mister Caleb." She set her hand atop the head of each child as she rattled off their names. "Emmie Jo and Joy June, you already met. This 'un here is Hank."

There was something about the girls that niggled at him — had since he first laid eyes on them.

He stood stock-still helplessly staring at them. Emmie Jo tugged on his pant leg to offer him a soul-stopping *hey*. The light in her green eyes sparkled like Millie's.

He dropped down to her eye level, then stuck out his hand and solemnly shook hers, muttering, "Mighty pleased to see y'all again, missy."

Emmie Jo giggled. "My name's not Missy, Mister 'Leb."

Caleb chuckled over his mispronounced name, delighted by her lisp. *She's as cute as the dickens.* "Oh, sorry about that. You must be Lady Jane of Spain. I see Lady Isadora is with y'all."

Emmie Jo beamed. "He called me Lady, Mama. He silly."

Joy June put her chubby little hands over her mouth to squelch her giggles.

Millie flushed at her girls' antics, then paled when she seemed to catch him taking a second look at Emmie Jo and Joy

June. She spoke in a rush. "Things have been mighty hard lately. Herman's working out of Alcoa in the plant, and even so, with all these young'uns, we need the money. Did Miss Emma Jean tell you I'm a-comin' out to do some cookin' at the Lodge full time? Ma's gonna watch the young'uns so's I can."

That made Caleb stand and take notice fast. "Uh, no . . . That, uh, that's good. Aunt Emma Jean can use the help. I'm leaving the Lodge."

She blanched. "Oh? I didn't hear . . . I mean, Miss Emma didn't say nuthin' about you leavin'." She looked him straight in the eye. "Y'all leavin' the Lodge because of me?"

Caleb just looked at her, trying his best to be casual. "Like I said, high time for me to move on. Everyone else has."

"Where you goin'?"

"Upcountry."

She raised a brow in question. "Backcountry?"

"No. Upcountry. As in up Mount LeConte."

"LeConte is so far away. Won't you be lonely?" Resignation laced her tone.

He straightened. "All I need is three hots and a cot. With all the hikers climbing up, I'll be busy enough I 'spect. There's a crew I'll be part of, too. I've had to make do in the past. Won't be no different there. You take care now. Nice running into ye." He packed up his gear, got his stringer of fish, and made to leave.

Suddenly, a little imp called out, "Let me see."

Caleb turned at the request from a little redhead — the spittin' image of Millie, except for the hair — splashing through the sparklingly clear water. Her eyes, all aglow with awe, really pulled on his bruised and wary heartstrings.

"Me, too," little Hank begged.

Emmie Jo and Joy June pleaded, "Can we touch 'em? Puhleeze."

The pleas of Millie's kids made him pause long enough to

show off his catch.

*Eww* and *Yuck* were the twins' assessments, but the little boy's eyes popped. Caleb had to admit he had an impressive catch of Mountain Brook Brown trout.

Millie nodded." Y'all loved hiking these hills . . . I remember our senior class hike up there."

Caleb remembered it, too. He had been glad Amy Rae was with him to distract him from the sight of Herman's class ring on the finger of Millie's left hand and Herman's adoring eyes laser-focused on her. At the time, Caleb had entertained the group with his harmonica. When he played, he forgot everything and everyone around him, letting himself get lost in the zone. His classmates had said he played the tired out of their exhausted muscles. Hiking up Mount LeConte was not for lightweights.

*Millie's eyes were so bright that afternoon, shining with that special glint in her eyes. The green in them, greener than new leaves in spring when they first burst through. I like me dem green eyes.*

Then the brunt of what Caleb had told Millie hit him hard. He'd just announced a commitment he'd have to make true. His decision, while spontaneous, was really the result of his growing restlessness. *But dammit, Millie looks mighty good. Good enough to . . . Fuck a damned duck. I'm outta here.* This time, he actually did tip his hat—his fishin' hat—and strode away.

Caleb wasn't sure, but Millie had looked shaken by his news. However, he was happy with his sudden decision. He would no longer have to worry about running into Millie. She was far too busy with her passel of kids anyway. *It don't matter none if she reacted to my movin' or not. Millie's in my past. I'm all about my future.*

# CHAPTER SEVEN: RAMBLING MAN

Mid-1980s

Time for Jacob Weathers had run out. Uncle Jacob died. While not completely unexpected since his first heart attack back in '69, his death still shook Caleb to his core.

For Caleb, Uncle Jacob had always been *Uncle Jake*. As a toddler, he couldn't get the *ob* sound out, but the *ache* part was easy since it was how he felt after his parents' untimely deaths and how he felt now. He wondered if Uncle Jake had felt sad because he hadn't called his uncle by that title since his boyhood. Uncle Jake had been the only father he knew. He'd been too young to remember much of his pa and ma.

John had Jacob's loss to cope with. John was picking up the pieces of his shattered world, though. Caleb figured it was high time for him to do so, too.

He took John aside after the funeral. "This place needs more help, John. I know you're doing all you can, but you should hire someone extra. Your ma needs more help even with you and Millie here." They were in a pickle, like Auntie Em often proclaimed.

John took a long look at him. "How you gonna be with Millie around all the time?"

Caleb and John had never been less than straight with each other. There was no reason to beat around the bush now.

"I don't think I can manage seein' her all the time. Thinking on headin' out of here. Y'all thinkin' that's cowardly?"

John doubled over with a belly laugh. "Me? Hell no, man!

Until I walk in your boots, I reckon I got no call to tell you how to tie your laces."

Caleb finally convinced John they needed more help, and he hired Pat, an old trusted family friend. She had helped keep the books at the Lodge during their peak seasons and had enough experience to run the place.

Caleb handled his grief by roaming the trails in the Great Smoky National Park. In no time, he had an impressive number of them under his belt. He was often accompanied by Hugh Robertson as he wandered the backcountry. Caleb would tease Hugh that he was coming around the Lodge to see Pat, not meet up with him and that Hugh should get up the nerve to ask her out.

Hugh did better than that. Not long after Caleb's teasing, Hugh dated Pat, courted her quick, and then straight up married her. Hugh's days as a widower had ended when he fell under Pat's spell, and the man started calling Caleb a mountain matchmaker. *Sure, sure. I can match everybody else but not myself. I need some of that zing thing Millie knew so much about.*

Caleb continued his treks through the wilderness. Sometimes Hugh would tag along when Pat was too busy with the Lodge. Most times, Caleb hiked on his own.

*Hiking through these mountains makes me feel God's presence. My mountain treks soothe my soul like rock-n-roll does for Bob Seeger. I couldn't find more truth in the man's words than entering this towering tree-lined temple. Glen Campbell expressed his feelings about the Appalachian Mountain chain in his song, West Virginia. Too bad Millie has become someone else's mountain mama.*

Caleb sat alone, letting the magic of the mountains saturate and rejuvenate his soul. He pulled out his harmonica and played peaceful melodies, the notes soulful and gut-wrenching. His mournful and agonizing losses throbbed through his music to uncover his broken places.

Auntie Em claimed the cracks in his soul were there to let the healing light shine in. "You can't see the stars unless it's dark."

He felt he was getting a double whammy of grief when Uncle Jake's recent death bled through the notes of the music he played.

Moved beyond words, he began to play *How Great Thou Art* and followed that with *America the Beautiful*. The birds' song accompanied his, then they were joined by the dulcet tones of someone he had heard sing karaoke at Bar None. *I know that voice. I've heard it before.* The voice belonged to a beautiful auburn-haired girl. He didn't know if she were ahead of him or behind him. It didn't matter. If they were meant to meet, they would. If not, then the time wasn't right. Caleb continued to play his harmonica, the notes sailing on the breeze to the chorus of the trees.

Something was calling Caleb. He was growing more and more restless. His *real* life had to start sometime, but he needed to find his path forward. In some ways, he was waiting for his turn. That responsibility he couldn't lay at Millie's or John's or even Jacob's doors. Caleb's life was *his* to make, and he had put it off for far too long.

Caleb had explored all the Quiet Walkways on both the Tennessee and North Carolina sides of the Park. They were short and self-guiding trails, each special in its own right and some harder than they looked.

He had a hard time restraining Tater — who somehow managed to escape the Lodge and find him whenever he went hiking. He once found her hidden away inside his backpack. He still had a hard time figuring how she managed that and how he missed the fact she had bummed a ride.

While dogs were permitted on Oconaluftee River Trail and Gatlinburg Trail, they weren't allowed on most hikes. Yet somehow, Tater always ended up finding him despite all the bells, whistles, and leashes he used to keep her home. *Shoulda named her Tramp for all the trapsin' she's done and miles she's walked. Or Rover, that'd fit, too.*

Whenever Caleb found Tater following him, he tried to teach her it was wrong. But her wagging tail and sparkling eyes betrayed her adoration and melted his heart. He'd ruffled the fur covering her head and ears. He just knew she comprehended her actions, and her dogged determination to be with him carried her over hill, dale, rill, and hollow. Privately, he admired Tater's spunk but knew Senior Ranger Scraper would only look the other way so many times.

One time, Tater even climbed to the summit of Mount LeConte and didn't emerge until the last steep trek of that hike, and *he* was the one who hid her in the backpack. Somehow, his precious, precocious pup knew when, where, and how to keep quiet. He loved his pooch. She always made him smile, bringing sunshine to his day and following him everywhere. If asked, he'd deny it, but truth be told, he had transferred his deep feelings for Millie to Tater.

He learned as much as he could about the trails, local lore, flora, and fauna he encountered on his walkabouts. His heroes were John Muir, Horace Kephart, and Wiley Oakley, who had forged the paths throughout the area. Ol' Wiley — often called the *Will Rogers of the South* or the *Roamin' Man of the Mountains* — was Caleb's secret idol. Caleb read everything he could get his hands on about the man. Wiley's personal history spoke to Caleb like none other.

Wiley's ma died tragically when he was a nine-year-old boy. Trying to comfort a young child, his relatives told him his ma was likely an angel. Upon hearing that, he spent hours wandering the Smoky Mountains and climbing the tallest peaks, hoping to catch sight of his ma's streaming robe in the white puffy clouds and her glittering crown in the constellations.

Wiley eventually became a local legendary wilderness guide, sharing his love of the Smoky Mountains with hunters, fishermen, and the like. Turned out Wiley was a renowned storyteller as well, even telling his tales on radios across America. The man was the perfect candidate for Caleb's much-needed hero.

Caleb figured maybe he could become as good a storyteller as Wiley, what with all the wandering he'd done. Auntie Em would encourage him when folks gathered around the fire pit for a bonfire at the Lodge.

"Tell us a tale," Auntie Em would say.

Word spread, and more and more folks hunched close together to listen to his sonorous voice telling his tales. Truth be told, even Millie brought her kids whenever she could to hear what Auntie Em called Caleb's Fireside Tales and Lore.

Caleb liked to recount many of Wiley's stories, his favorite being what Wiley called *The Cow Barn*. He always retold it as close as he could to Wiley's own telling, ending it with, "Newly married young folks need to build them a cow barn to save the peace and a passel of trouble."

Caleb wished he'd had that chance with Millie.

In addition to Wiley's tales, Caleb enjoyed repeating stories from his own stock of mountain lore. Soon, he was almost as popular as his hero, Wiley Oakley.

Had Caleb gone to college, he'd ofttimes said he probably would have looked into Appalachian history and heritage, forestry, tourism, or some such. As it was, Caleb aimed to be a trail guide at the very least, like his hero before him. He continued to tell his tales to anyone who'd listen and even regaled the Lodge staff. He was proud to share his mountain heritage and often introduced newbies to the many trails weaving their way through the hills. Frequently, he told his audience about his own adventures. He was truly done hiking the Chimney Tops Trail. Caleb winked. "I hate that gap at the top of the trail. I hiked that trail five times too many. That's enough. I heard the tree talk whisper nooo gooo." He smiled. "I'm smart enough to heed their warning. Now, if the right, purdy girl wants to see those pinnacles, don't be too surprised iffen ye see me up there alongside her." It was taking him a long while to move on because he had himself emotionally frozen in time.

*I'd hike it for Millie in a heartbeat — tree talk or not. We always ended up doin' more kissin' than hikin'. I'd bet we'd never even make it to the trailhead.*

# CHAPTER EIGHT: GOING UP COUNTRY

1986

One day while hiking, Caleb reviewed several conversations he'd had with his Uncle Jake, who had known the LeConte Lodge founders personally. Caleb had met Jack Huff and figured maybe the man could help get him out of Elkmont—away from Millie.

After the last leg strenuous trail up LeConte, he ran into his hikin' buddy, Hugh Robertson, chatting with two men outside the building. Hugh introduced Caleb to Jim Huff—Jack's nephew—and Hugh Ogle. The two had recently bought the lodge.

After a quick *hey* greeting, Hikin' Hugh smiled at Caleb. "Y'all hankerin' to take the job up here? They can use the help."

Caleb, slightly taken aback, replied, "Jist might be. It'd be perfect timing."

Jim hooked his fingers underneath his bib overalls and tilted his head. "Look healthy. Betcha could lift thirty pounds."

Caleb nodded and flexed his bicep. "Sure could."

There was a twinkle in Jim's gaze, his eyes narrowing, sizing him up. "But are ye up to dealin' with the latrines?"

Caleb frowned but again nodded. "I guess I could."

Jim considered him for a moment. "Can ye stand yer own company iffen you stayed over the winter?"

Caleb chuckled. "I could."

Hikin' Hugh chimed in. "He gits along with folks and could charm the fleece off a sheep. He got innkeepin' in his blood what with his experience workin' the Lodge down Elkmont. Plus, he knows the backcountry well enough."

"Iffen yer interested, jist say so. Can ye fix living with no *eee*electricity? Come to that are ye handy?"

A slow smile crossed Caleb's face as he devised his response. He recalled make-out sessions with Millie, Amy Rae, and Dede, but he was fairly sure that was not the kind of *handy* his prospective employer was looking for. "Yep. Can do."

Tater's vigorous and loud bark had Caleb turning to see his pooch running the last few feet to be by his side. She wagged her tail, gazed up at him with her adoring amber eyes, and panted with her tongue lolling out the side of her mouth. He shook his head at her following him up the mountain *again*. The men laughed and dubbed her their Mount LeConte Mascot.

"Looks like your dog settled it." Hugh chuckled.

Anyone who knew anything knew there was no way Tater'd let Caleb soldier on alone.

Jim leaned back on his heels, thumbs still hooked under his bib overalls as he thought some. "How's yer 'rithmatic?"

Caleb grinned. "Good, I reckon. Got through school okay."

Jim smiled. "That so? Some figurin' comes up fer guests."

Caleb nodded. "Ah know."

After his last encounter with Millie and her brood, Caleb decided then and there to work at LeConte Lodge a season and see how he liked it. There'd be a steady crew and frequent guests, so he knew he wouldn't be lonely. Plus, he had Tater.

He flashed Jim a smile. "Consider me your new hire."

The men slapped him on the back and walked him over to the LeConte Lodge manager to begin what paperwork there was.

Caleb let out a heavy sigh of relief. He'd told Millie he was goin' upcountry to work, and now he'd cinched the deal.

All he had said to Millie about going upcountry, along with his talk with John about seeing Millie every day, had served as his wake-up call. *The torture of seeing Millie is too damn much. Havin' kids hasn't hurt her figure none, either. She looks hot and happy, but I can't take that kind of happiness on a daily basis. Which means one of us has to skedaddle. That means me. Gotta hold the shot and let the coon go free.*

With John and Pat helping Auntie Em, Caleb was needed less and less at the Lodge even after Uncle Jacob's death. His cousin worked the place and began developing the Gatlinburg Crafts Community. Pat had several years of working the Lodge under her belt and was helping Auntie Em manage and run the Lodge. So he was free to follow his legacy to the LeConte Lodge.

He'd be starting his new job in a couple of days. The season usually ran from March through the end of November at the LeConte Lodge. It seemed like those dates had become as reliable as milk going sour after too long in the sun.

Caleb knew he'd better talk to Emma Jean before Millie said something. His aunt was considered a *granny woman* now, wise in the ways few were. He respected her and owed her that much. He hadn't told his aunt of his talk of moving upcountry, but he knew *he* better be the one to tell Auntie Em about working the summer at LeConte Lodge.

That very night he approached his aunt, and even the breeze seemed to encourage his decision. "Auntie Em, it's time I move on."

Emma Jean's brow lifted. "How so? You hear Millie's comin' to work full time this summer?" Then she laughed. "Look, Caleb, it's written all over you. You're a grown man now. I can't expect you to stay here forever and help out any longer. You have your own life to live. I've got help with John and Pat."

Time had passed him by as fast as the chain saws cutting through timber back when lumbering was big business in Elkmont. Everyone else his age had long since moved on, and it was clearly time he did, too.

"As I said afore, it's time you live your own life," Emma Jean continued. "Word around here is you might be making LeConte Lodge your home . . . year-round."

He nodded and paused a moment, thoughtful. "Ah aim to feel it out first. See how I like it, then decide."

Emma Jean stared at him and raised a brow. "Should I make some city chicken and greens for your last supper here?"

He chuckled. "Thanks. But I'm going out for my last hurrah. I'll grab a burger."

"Gonna paint the town red? Y'all be careful of those high steppin' women, hear me?"

Caleb smothered a laugh. "Haven't met any so far."

Emma Jean cocked her head, then peered over her glasses. "I have a hunch that'll change. It's way past time you stop moonin' over Millie."

He gave her a hug. "Millie who?"

She swatted his rear end with her dishtowel.

Caleb chuckled, shook his head, and headed for his room. *Auntie Em has an Irishwomen's instincts. Some say she has the sight and can see straight through both the past and the future. She sure gets me right.*

He dressed in a nice shirt and new jeans, then splashed on some clean pine-scented cologne and headed out the door. *Wonder if I'll catch sight of that auburn-haired vixen who's been stealin' into my dreams lately? What's her name? Colleen? Maxine? Kathleen? Sunmthin' 'leen if my memory serves me right. Saw her dancin' up a storm last time I stepped out.*

On the far side of town — out some distance — Caleb pulled

his Ford pickup outside the Bar None tavern. Gatlinburg was in a dry county, and only the locals knew about this roadhouse. It had operated forever, since way back in the old days. Back then, if the pickle barrel was outside on the porch, it meant the revenuers were around, so *don't come to sell or buy moonshine.* Over time, the pickle barrel was seldom outside. It still urged caution—just in case.

The place was hopping, and he could hear the country music blaring and the sound of people having a good time as he looked for a parking spot. He threw his truck into park and looked at the orange light bleeding out through the windows, welcoming the partiers. A red neon sign labeled the bar and the white glow of the jukebox added to whatever ambiance the dive had. It looked to be packed to the rafters with revelers ready for some dancin', he reckoned. He could hear folks clappin', back slappin', and hootin' and hollerin'.

Sometimes singers took the mic and sang karaoke—everything from ole time gospel, blues, country, as well as rock-n-roll tunes. It was rumored that the Oak Ridge Boys sang there every now and then, as did various members of the Carter family. No one ever knew who would show up, but one thing was certain, they'd have a good time at Bar None. When the local band took a break, the jukebox took over.

As he entered the bar, he immediately spotted the auburn-haired vixen he had seen in the past, laughing over a foaming mug of beer. Soon she set the mug down, and some dude Texas two-stepped her around the wooden floorboards. Caleb continued to watch as she seemed to accept a different man's offer each time a new song came on.

The jukebox switched to play Roberta Flack's *The First Time Ever I Saw Your Face,* and some*thing,* some unseen force, propelled Caleb to her side. He tapped the guy she was dancing with on the shoulder and cut in. She laughed, and fortunately, the fellow backed off graciously—a real miracle.

She smiled up at him as they swayed on the dance floor. "My name's Jolene. And y'all's?"

Caleb leaned into her, winked, and said, "I'm the man you been lookin' for. How 'bout we just hush and enjoy this dance."

She cocked a brow at him and laughed. "Ain't possible to shut me up."

He bent his head, stole a glance, and saw a *yes* in her gaze. "I bet I know how."

There was a challenge in her look. "Do tell."

Caleb bent his mouth and kissed her red, lush lips.

She laughed. "Bless your heart, guess I have to eat my words."

Jolene, a gleam in her eyes, danced with him again and again. When Nancy Sinatra's *These Boots Are Made for Walkin'* played, he got a kick outta her spunk as she got into the lyrics, stompin' her cowboy boots as she danced.

Caleb liked this shiny-headed long-haired pale-skinned woman. He almost laughed when she took the mic and signaled the band to play Loretta Lynn's *You Ain't Woman Enough* after she warded off a wannabe contender for Caleb's attention. The gal got the message. If it came to a catfight, his money was on Jolene. That gleam in her eyes was fierce. Anyone with half a brain would be wise to back out of her radar.

They spent the rest of the night dancing under the low lights of the smoke-filled bar. When other men approached, Jolene just waved them off and kept dancing with Caleb. He'd never enjoyed dancing like he did with her. A sparkle reflected in her eyes, and she seemed as enchanted as he. Good thing, since his gaze kept straying to her full, high breasts, and her tight skinny jeans stretched over a fit ass. The air felt filled with magic, and a cool breeze wafted through the open screen windows, sighing a musical *ohhh yeahhhh*. Had Tater been there, she'd have no doubt woofed in approval.

The tempo of the night moved from the foot stoppin' to slow dancin' to Patsy Kline's *Crazy*, and Caleb wondered for the first time in years if he wasn't just a little crazy, too—about *Jolene*. They ended the night kissing to the tune *There Goes My Everything*.

"I'd be happy to drive you home . . ." Caleb offered. "Unless you're in mind for sumthin' more. Night's young."

"Ain't no need, I have my bike. Gotta get up with the sun. I got plans."

"Those plans could include—"

"I'm no honky-tonk ho, honey."

"Breakfast." He laughed. "So there, missy, my motives were pure as freshly fallen snow."

Jolene grinned. "I'd say *see ye around*, but I have a trip up Trillium Gap Trail early tomorrow mornin'. I've been scoping out the trails 'round here lately. I hear tell there's some lodge up there." She winked." Maybe I'll get a job there."

Caleb played along. "You don't say? Maybe I'll see ye then."

She laughed. "Maybe you will. Maybe you won't." She peered at him as if measuring him, sizing up his potential. "You look hardy enough."

Surprise shocked him, and the beer in his mouth sprayed everywhere, luckily missing Jolene. Caleb said his goodbyes and left the tavern.

# Chapter Nine: On Top of Old Smoky

The next morning, Caleb decided to take the Alum Cave route up Mount LeConte. He set off with a backpack full of jeans, underwear, socks, and an extra pair of boots. He'd also packed his own toiletries, towels, and washcloths, because the rustic lodge had no private amenities. He included the pocketknife and compass Uncle Jake had given him when he'd made his Confirmation. He threw in some trail guides and the St. Joseph Bible Auntie Em gave him, too. He knew he would probably return to Elkmont about eight times throughout the operating season, so he could always restock if needed.

The trail got dicey in a few areas as it climbed even though the weather was balmy for March and no ice glaze was present. Caleb was secure in his knowledge of this trail and happy for the hard work of the Civilian Conservation Corps back in the 1930s, carving a path from the mountain rock itself.

The sun rose and shone brightly by the time he reached the laurel thicket just beyond the bluff a piece. He stopped there for his lunch. Auntie Em had made him several country ham sandwiches and included a cherry popover for dessert. In addition, he carried a baggie of trail mix, and his canteen provided the water he'd need for the scenic trek. He'd decided to maintain a steady leisurely pace since he wasn't expected until dinnertime.

He'd committed to work the summer season and maybe stay on. LeConte Lodge closed in November, so after the season ended, he'd see whether he'd accept the position as winter caretaker. It was simply too soon to make that decision.

Caleb let his mind wander as he sauntered up the mountainside. With no showers at the lodge, a sponge bath was as good as it got for staff and guests alike. He'd heard that in the past, some aromatic crew members would hike down the trail for a more complete wash-up at Rainbow Falls on their days off. These days, crew members typically decided that it made more sense to go home for a hot shower and a soft familiar bed.

Thinking of the falls sent Caleb's fantasies on a whirlwind. He imagined Jolene's high breasts and tight ass glistening under the falls' shower of cold mountain water, the icy spray forcing her nipples to tighten and pucker. He pictured her impaled on his shaft, her legs embracing his torso, her warm lips on his, and her hands all over him. He hoped to try that with Jolene in the real world, real soon. Judging by the dance in his pants, the sooner, the better. He felt sure things seemed to be headed in that direction.

Caleb figured a wonderful perk to *his* new job could include hiring and then tiring Jolene out by means of prolonged heavy breathing and red-hot sex. To him, she was everything sensual. She appeared to be a free spirit who enjoyed the men who flocked around her. He wanted to be the one who got lucky. He yearned and burned for a happy ending.

He shook off his fantasies and thought about his upcoming job. He knew enough carpentry from maintaining the Sugarlands Lodge, so he knew he'd be up to the task of becoming a worthy staff member. There was no electricity up there, nor indoor plumbing in the cabins, but that was no biggie. Plumbing was a headache anyway, so he was glad he only had to worry about cleaning the few separate guest bathrooms.

He heard the dinner bell ringing as he finally reached the entrance to LeConte Lodge. He entered the Dining Hall and was greeted by the smiling faces of the other staff members. His day ended with a hearty meal and pleasant conversation in what was to be his home for the foreseeable future.

Caleb's first task had been to help manage and stock the inventory that came up by helicopter at the beginning of the season. That supply drop carried enough to last the lodge for the season and beyond. He took to it like wild geese took to the sky. He knew he would be carrying additional personal items up when he made his treks down to town.

After a few days, he learned his time off would be on a rotating basis, and he could go down the mountain with the other crew members heading for a break. In the meantime, he did the grunt work he was assigned, which he found out — quickly — did include latrine maintenance. Plus, he helped out with the unpacking and packing of supplies, laundry, bedding, and trash that was hauled up and down the mountain three times each week using horses.

Each day's work began by preparing a hearty breakfast with the crew and ended by lighting kerosene lamps in each cabin at night. He learned to use old newspapers to clean the lantern globes each morning. He didn't enjoy the sooty job but carried it out with his usual good cheer. He was also responsible for igniting the available propane heaters against the cool nights. It didn't take long for him to learn his tasks and carry them out efficiently.

His lonely nights fueled his Jolene fantasies. He'd never imagined Amy Rae or Dede that way. And he almost never thought of Millie anymore because all he could recall were a few memories getting to third base with her. He had moved far beyond that.

Caleb quickly became indispensable at the lodge. He could

fix anything, cook, clean, make beds, and keep the seven single cabins and additional group cabins immaculate.

Within a short time, he found mountain top living buoyed him. He felt alive and virile and at peace. Especially the times he escorted groups of intrepid hikers to Myrtle Point to watch the sunrise or Cliff Top to see the sunset. Those events were always awe-inspiring for him.

On the outside, he was a rugged mountain man. On the inside, he became a poet. He had always had the soul of a music man whose art was revealed in music and his storytelling. After moving to LeConte, he began recording his experiences and feelings in poems—usually in blank verse—and often drew illustrations to accompany them. Poetry took up residence in his soul right alongside his fiddling. After sharing some with his fellow staff members, they encouraged him to sell them as souvenirs in their small gift shop.

Most often, the long hikes and the fresh air tuckered out guests who were prone to rising with the sun and shutting down with the sun. The day's rhythm matched the tempo of the breezes that caressed the hills in good times and raged fiercely during storms. This day, it blew as gently as Millie's kisses. But it wasn't really Millie's kisses that captured his attention now. It was that fiery one he'd shared with that minx, Jolene, who stole into his thoughts more and more lately. It wasn't all that long ago that she'd proved herself a mighty good kisser. He wondered if she had been serious that night when she said she was getting up early to climb LeConte. She'd mentioned checking out the lodge, but he hadn't seen her around.

Then one morning, he was in the Dining Hall sipping his coffee, and she walked in, carefree as ever. She paused in the doorway for a moment, then approached him with a smile.

"Fancy meeting you here," she greeted.

He poured a mug of hot mountain-grown coffee handed it

to her. When she reached for it, their hands touched, and a frisson of heat sizzled up his arm.

She cleared her throat. "Don't mind if I do. Y'all have sugar? Honey?"

He winked as he leaned against the counter, coffeepot still in his hands. "You are all the sweet that coffee needs."

She laughed. "That's lame. What am I supposed to do? Stir it with my finger?"

Caleb pointed to the honeypot sitting on the nearby table.

Jolene smiled her pleasure and drizzled some honey into the blend. She blew on the coffee to cool it. Then she sat, loosened the laces in her well-broken-in hiking boots, and stretched her long legs out in front of her.

He nodded, impressed that her clothing and footwear seemed to be premium quality.

Jolene apparently noticed him surveying her outfit and chuckled. "Surprised I know how to dress for the mountain weather? Sudden temperature changes, spring in the hills, storms, I got it. I always layer up and use proper gear. It is the wilderness, after all. I am all about survival, and ye know what they say, *cotton kills*."

He smiled his admiration. "I'm beginning to see that you're a seasoned outdoorsman."

Jolene slowly exhaled as she drawled, "Watch your nouns now. As you no doubt have noticed, I'm all woman, and we respect the outdoors and environment as much as anyone."

He squinted in her direction, watching her closely, checking carefully. "You one of them *libbers*?"

She spat out her coffee, laughing. "I don't think of myself that way. I'm a person who's prepared. I've spent my whole life outside. I've worked and hiked in the Rockies, and Outfitters Incorporated—I work with them—are looking to spread its reach down here."

He cocked a brow. "So, y'all on the job? On the clock as we

say."

She grinned. "Yup, I am."

His gaze intent, he spoke, "In what capacity?"

She gave him a long look in return and said, "I'm a site scout this minute, but if we set up here, I'll be a *llama mama*."

It was Caleb's turn to spit out his coffee. "A what?"

"I'm a llama wrangler. What do you do?"

He cocked a brow. "Llama wrangler? Seriously?"

Jolene nodded and continued undaunted. "I'm fixin' to discuss using a llama train instead of horses or mules your management hires to supplement the helicopter supply drops. I'm here to propose it with management over lunch."

Caleb grinned. "You can proposition me."

"Hardee har har. That would be a snap."

"I like your confidence. Seriously, show me what ye got. Consider it practice for your proposal."

She straightened and cleared her throat and began her pitch. "I'm Jolene from Outfitters Inc. My company can replace your pack horses with ecofriendly llamas. We can make supply runs using llamas that are not only cost effective but equally good for the environment."

Caleb leaned across the space between them. "I work the LeConte Lodge and will welcome you and your . . . er . . . llamas any time. In fact, I'm the cook for today making said lunch. I find the idea fascinating. You shore are sumthin', gal. *Llama mama*, that's rich. A new one on me."

"Technically, I'm *officially* a llama *wrangler*, but I specialize in the administrative marketing for our corporation, too."

He straightened his stance, interested in the role and in her. "So, llama wrangling is your thing?"

"It is." She raised her wrist to show him a small llama tattoo inked above the joint. "But you'll have to excuse me. I see my business contacts have arrived. I'll catch ye later before I trek down. Afterward, I'll tell you all about wrangling lla-mas." She winked.

He looked up, and sure enough, several people were head-ing straight for them, including Tim Line, the lodge manager, Jim Huff, and Hugh Ogle. Caleb seated them and then left them to talk while he began preparing their food. After all, it was his turn for cooking. He also had to get food ready for the hungry guests. In fact, he could already see a small crowd awaiting the clang of the old brass triangle.

Caleb overheard the conversation as he placed a platter of sandwiches on the table. He decided to stay in the open area of the dining room to keep an eye and ear on the meeting.

Jim gave a grunt approval. "Miss Jolene, I'm fixin' to lend an ear to what you have to say, but I like horses. Word is ye like alpacas or some such."

Jolene smiled but didn't correct his referring to alpacas in-stead of llamas.

Jim continued. "We've been using horses for the past sixty years. Why on earth would we use llamas all of a sudden?"

Jolene kept her smile in place. "I get that. How's that work-ing out for you?"

Tim's brow furrowed in concentration. "Well, it can create problems with the NPS rangers. They are concerned with trail erosion and suchlike."

Jim snorted. "Damned horseshit bothers the hikers, and there's re-shoeing them. Might be time to try sumthin' new."

Caleb set down a pitcher of Sweet Tea. He had to stifle a chuckle at Jim's expression.

Jolene nodded. "And the cost?"

Tim leaned in. "Expensive. Pack animals, feed, and vet ex-penses not to mention stabling them. Adds up fast."

Jolene seized the moment. "Llamas have been used in the Himalayas for transport for centuries. Llamas are cheap. They don't require barns and they don't have hooves or shoes tearing up the environment. Did I mention they are cheaper than dirt?"

Jim grunted. "But can they carry the weight?"

Jolene rattled the facts off. "Each llama can pack in or out up to sixty pounds — some seventy pounds, depending on the size of the llama and the cargo. Their saddle bags last long, too."

"I heard they spit and hiss," Hugh commented. "We ain't trained for 'em. Cost a heap to do that. Pry hafta hire in new hands."

Jolene smiled. "I hear that so often I wish I had a dollar each time. I'd be rich. That's almost a myth. I haven't heard any hissing, but they do spit. But mostly they hum, because they are restless and want to get the job done, or they're showing another llama who's dominate. If you respect them and use a modulated tone, they'll prove easy to live and work with."

Caleb came back with more coffee and heard Jolene offer them a look at her prospectus. He saw the respect in the old mountaineers grow with each statement she made, but when they saw her glow with pride over her company's llamas that seemed to seal the deal.

She spoke warmly about the llamas she worked. "Coal is all black and his strength is as good as any bull. Daisy is strong but sweet. Ellen loves the lead position. I'll be using a different team but I love them all. They're hard workers. Don't get me wrong. You don't treat them as pets or like humans but give them a task, a trail, a kind tone, and a pancake and they'll serve you well at half the cost and care. We have even used old abandoned school buses to house them. So, it's a good deal." She munched on a piece of a huge homemade chocolate chip cookie. "I can subcontract with y'all and train the staff you have. Plus, I have my own llama team you can rent or own."

Tim looked at her clearly surprised. "What's that? These 'uns?"

"It only takes about four hours to train llama wranglers, and I can get Caleb up to speed fast. I can get a llama train here for a sample run, too, if you'd like." She gave Caleb a wink as she spoke to the decision-makers of the LeConte Lodge.

"Seriously?" Caleb interjected.

Jolene nodded. "Do statues in the south face north?"

He nodded. "Yeah. Never turn your back on the north."

She wore a smug smile. "I rest my case."

Jolene addressed her remarks to Tim. "It'll take a few weeks to get back to Colorado, find the right team, and transport the llamas." She winked. "Or y'all contract for my team, if you're interested."

"Shake on it, li'l lady," Jim said after getting a quick nod from Tim. "Ah think ah'll work up a subcontract."

"Perfect." Jolene smiled. "A subcontract will work both for me and Outfitters Inc. It's the best of both worlds."

Caleb was amazed she didn't bristle at Jim's faux pas, calling her *li'l lady*. But—truth be told—he nearly shit himself when he heard her mention his name.

Jolene put out her hand. She shook hands all around.

Billy Bo Bean teased him mercilessly once he was back in the kitchen. His being volunteered got him a lot of ribbing from the other crew members, who saw it as her wanting the chance to get time with him. But it made Caleb think. He had no interest in working with the llama train, but as a llama wrangler and the chance to work with Jolene, he could seriously get into that.

Caleb's job responsibilities kept him busy until dinnertime. Then he was back in the kitchen, serving roast beef, mashed potatoes and gravy, and southern style green beans with pork belly to the guests. Toward the end of the meal, he spied Jolene at a table for four and decided to join her. Most folks had cleared out by then, so his work was done for the evening.

Jolene insisted that he share another huge chocolate chip cookie with her claiming, "These carbs will overload my system. Help a gal out here." Then she batted her eyes and puckered her lips.

He caved and grabbed half the cookie.

"That was easy." She chuckled.

He grinned. "A man would have to be plumb dumb to say no to a gal like you. I don't rightly aim to play hard to get."

She grinned. "Here I went and thought you were a roaming, ramblin' mountain man, trying hard to escape the desperate clutch of a single woman and her wiles. All intent to roam—"

Caleb smiled as he slowly took in her frame. "I roam hills and hollows."

She puffed out her chest. "Didn't I just say that? I was right."

"That ye are."

Jolene looked at him and winked. "Maybe someday you just might get lucky, but right now, I gotta git." Jolene leaned forward and gave him a lingering, luscious goodbye kiss full on his lips.

Caleb swore his toes curled in his sturdy boots and knew for a fact another part of him rose rapidly in response.

Later that evening, after the nightly trek of newcomers to Cliff Top to watch the sunset, Caleb returned to his cabin with his head full of Jolene. The sight of her. The smell. The feel. The thrill. All screamed full blast. He was interested, all right. To distract himself, his thoughts focused on her smarts, not her parts. Not her lips. Not her hips. Not her mouth. *No, I'm not thinkin' on any of that. Her brain, man. Get your mind off her body.*

To help, he latched on to thinking about Jolene's wilderness wear, which had impressed him. It certainly deepened her credibility. Not that he doubted she was a llama wrangler, but she certainly was more than a vacation hiker or thrill seeker.

Her waterproof jacket and over pants, as well as her wool socks peeking over her high-top laced boots, proved she was no glamper. He reckoned she'd be plenty comfortable in a sleeping bag with no need for a fancy-dancy cabin that passed for camping at several campsites out Dolly Parton Highway. No froufrou frills for that woman.

Jolene had also replenished her trail snacks and water, then checked her headlamp before hiking back down the mountain. Not something a rookie, much less a *girlie girl*, would likely do. She obviously knew what she was doing.

*Still, she put herself in danger by hiking alone.* The enormity of his thought hit him hard. *Hell, I hike alone, too, but I'm a . . . man?* Was he a closet male chauvinist pig? *I better practice what I preach. I am judging her choice just because she's a woman. Shiiit on a shingle. Where do I get off? Does Tater count as a hiking partner?* Wouldn't she go all *Lassie* on him and bring rescuers to him should he need it?

# Chapter Ten: She'll Be Comin' Round the Mountain

Several weeks later, the LeConte staff rotation placed Caleb in town. Jolene gave him directions to a farm she'd made arrangements with temporarily out Wears Valley to house the llamas. His training was about to begin, and he figured he'd do okay if he could ignore her trim body. If he didn't focus on her lush mouth. If he could control his errant cock.

He spied her right away. Her hair was tucked under an alpine print wool cap like those worn in the Andes or Himalayas. She looked surprisingly sexy in it.

Jolene had bent over to fiddle with some contraption or other — no doubt connected to llama equipment. Her rear end provided him with a world-class view of womanhood at its peak. It gave him a jolt. He struggled hard against the urge to grab her ass and give it a slap or at least a squeeze. His face heated when she turned and caught him staring.

She straightened and raised a brow. "Take a picture, it'll last longer."

His face heated even more, probably red as a beet.

She laughed. "Don't be so uptight. I'm messin' with ye. I'd be disappointed in you if you didn't take a gander. At least you didn't cop a feel."

His embarrassment deepened. *Geesh, can she read minds, too?*

She disappeared into a livestock trailer and led out a llama as white as winter snow. "Snow White, meet your Prince

Charming, Caleb." She led the animal to his left side.

Caleb gave a small laugh and took an involuntary step backward.

"Snow White won't bite ye." Jolene winked. "But I might."

She gave the llama a cube of something. "She's a real honey. Aren't ye?" She apparently caught his questioning look. "Alfalfa cubes. A treat. Nutritious but satisfying."

Reaching his hand out in front of him like he would when approaching a strange dog, he walked toward the llama.

Jolene warned, "Protect your fingers. Ball your fist. Let her get a good whiff first. She'll probably like your scent, I do."

He complied.

Jolene leaned closer and inhaled. "Whatcha wearing?"

"I'm au natural. Pure male." He winked, hoping it was a sexy one.

If women could purr, Jolene's response came close to it. She handed him a cube. "You give it to her this time."

He took the cube, still wary and unsure. "She won't bite me, will she?"

Jolene all but groaned. "Puh-leeze." She cocked a brow his way. "You plan to bite her? Mistreat her?"

He returned her look. "No. Of course not."

"Why not?"

He shifted his weight. "Why would I?"

She nodded. "Exactly. Treat her respectfully, and you'll be fine."

"Hmm. I thought for sure you'd give her sugar."

She snorted. "Because I like it? That doesn't mean it's good for her any more than it is for me."

He crooned as he held the treat to Snow White's mouth. "Here ye go, sweet lady. Aren't you a little cutie patootie?"

Jolene froze. "What are you doing?"

"Getting to know her is all."

"Then talk in a regular tone. Kids don't like baby talk, and she doesn't need it. R-e-s-p-e-c-t," she sang. "Don't bark. Don't yell. Just tell her what to do. Some gals don't need sweet talk. Some do."

"I see. Do y'all?"

She snorted. "Depends. Sometimes. Usually I prefer" —she bent to whisper in his ear— "talkin' dirty." She winked at him. "After you give her what she needs, check her coat."

Caleb looked at Snow White and smiled. "Lookin' good."

Jolene moved next to him to demonstrate, leaving precious little space between their bodies. "Like this." She ran her fingers lightly across his chest as if petting him. "See?"

He saw all right. He was getting hotter by the second.

"See these twigs? Leaves? Check for that, and especially, get the burrs out." She handed him a brush.

Their hands touched in the exchange, and Caleb could only stare.

Jolene didn't pull it away, nor did she move. After a few moments, when she did move, her ass hit his rod, and his manhood rose in response.

He turned his attention to the llama and noticed a burr on her thigh. He reached to pull it out.

Jolene waggled her fingers. "Prepare her first, remember?"

"Pardon me, Miss White, but you have a burr." The llama shifted but allowed his touch. Once it was freed, he began to brush her gently.

"That all ye got?" Jolene covered his hand with hers and bore down. "She's a lady, not a baby. Brush her like you mean it. You're not making love."

Wishing he and Jolene were, he mumbled, "Hafta do sumthin' about that sorry state of affairs."

His response might have seemed meek and mild, yet inside, hot blood rushed through his loins. He struggled to keep his mind on the task at hand.

"Yes, ma'am." He chuckled and brushed the llama using

sure steady pressure.

This time, Jolene smiled her approval. She winked and led Snow White away, then returned with a different llama.

He got a whiff of spice as Jolene passed him. The scent of her perfume got to him, causing his balls to tighten even more. He shook off his desire and moved closer to the next llama, still hesitant.

Jolene covered his hands with hers and guided his fingers over the warm coat of the animal. The llama shuffled and hummed.

Caleb's hot blood hummed, too. "What's she doing?"

Jolene winked and handed him a brush. "Enjoying. It's an anticipatory response. Now brush her."

Caleb got lost in daydreams as he tentatively stroked the llama's wooly coat.

"Again, you're not making love," Jolene said. "Add some pressure to your strokes."

Caleb stopped pretending he was stroking Jolene and applied a firmer touch to his brushing.

"Some of us females like a heavier touch."

He cocked a brow. "That right? I aim to please."

Jolene gave a chuckle. "I bet you do, too." She grabbed a blanket. "The blankets need to be checked for twigs and burrs first." She did so, then grabbed a saddle. "Each saddle is tailored for a specific animal. We let them smell it before we put it on their backs."

Caleb watched as she demonstrated how to cinch the saddle and the breast strap to the llama.

"We've prepacked the panniers—"

"Say what?"

"Saddlebags. They're full of perishable food, mail, and fresh linens. Tim gave us his usual order so you can get a real feel for this."

He nodded.

"Okay. We're going to add the panniers. This, though, is a two-person job. Meet Frank."

A tall, gangly man left the driver's side of the truck when she called to him. While Caleb watched, they hooked a pannier over two x shaped horns at the top of the saddle. Frank tied the llama to the tailer with the lead lines.

Jolene called out to Frank. "Bring Snow Balls out."

Caleb raised his brow in question.

Jolene caught his look. "What? He's a boy. Boys have balls."

Caleb exchanged a glance with Frank, and the corners of the man's mouth struggled against curling with whatever thoughts went through his head.

Jolene scowled at them both.

Caleb grinned. "I didn't say anything."

"You didn't have to. Frank, bring Balls here." Jolene snorted. "Grow up, you two."

Frank led another pure white llama out. "Meet Snow Balls, Snow White's son. You get him ready."

Caleb was feeling good about this. "Easy peasy." He let Balls sniff his hand, walked his fingers over him, checked his coat, brushed him, checked his blanket, placed the saddle, and cinched it as he'd been taught. Then he added the first pannier. The animal shifted and shied away. He fumbled a bit but managed to get the other on him with Frank's help.

Snow Balls promptly lay down and would not budge.

Caleb lifted his hat and scratched his head, perplexed. He had done everything right, so what went wrong? "What'd I do? Why is he lying down?"

When Jolene and Frank quit laughing, Jolene explained. "You forgot to *weigh* his saddlebag. Both panniers must weigh the same, or they won't carry the load."

"Don't rightly recall ye talkin' about weighing anything."

"Show him, Frank."

Frank took a handheld scale with a hook and lifted the bag. "Thirty pounds." Then he repeated the process with the other. "Thirty-two pounds." Then he took several rocks from the ground, added them to the first bag, then weighed it again. "Thirty-two pounds."

Jolene chuckled again—appearing proud of her prank—and walked over. "Every rookie makes some mistake."

He growled. "Shit on a shingle! You set me up."

She giggled. "Yep."

He laughed. "Keep me humble, huh?"

"Keep you sharp. Don't worry, we aren't taking him. Not good to mix the sexes together during a trek. Need to keep them separate. Get Lady now. Balls was just practice. Try again, Caleb."

He swore Snow White smiled at him. At least she didn't spit.

Caleb learned quickly, repeating the process with Lady, Betty, Beauty, Butterfly, and then Ebony.

He turned to Jolene, confused. "Why Ebony? She's all white."

Jolene grinned. "For fun. They like to mix it up."

He frowned. "And won't Butterfly get an identity crisis?"

Jolene shook her head. "No. Why would she?"

He shrugged. "With an insect for a name."

She sighed. "Rookies. Take a look at her markings."

Sure enough, a symmetrical dark patch of fur on her forehead looked remarkably like a butterfly. Butterfly headbutted him.

He stepped back a bit. "Hey, I'm sorry, sweetheart."

Jolene shook her head. "She's thirsty. That's what she's trying to tell ye."

Hands at his side, he nodded. "Riight. I'll get the water. Where's the bucket?"

"She'd pry kick it."

"Ye don't say? She'd drown then? How do they drink?"

"Bless your heart." Still shaking her head, she led him to the horse trough then winked. "Same way the horses drink. Or from the stream. I'm just joshing with ye. Couldn't resist saying she'd *kick the bucket*. By the way, she'd drink from a bucket, but the trough is fresh."

It took about an hour to load the seven llamas into the trailer and reach the trailhead. Before they embarked on the trek, Jolene walked up the line to whisper in the left ear of each llama and give them another alfalfa cube. Snow White was chosen for the lead position.

"Snow doesn't mind someone walking in front of her," Jolene explained. "You lead, since you know this trail so well."

Caleb took the line, shook it, and yelled, "Mush!"

The animals shifted nervously, beginning to bunch together.

"What the hell was that?" Jolene snapped.

"I'm getting them going."

She marched up and snatched the lead line from him. "Go to the rear of the line. Follow my lead." She started to walk, holding the lead line. The llama train — linked by five feet of rope between them — began their trek, following her like ducklings.

He stood there. "That's all you got?"

"That's all it takes."

"Where's the fun in that? The drama? The excitement?"

Jolene looked over her shoulder at him. "Trust me, llama drama you don't want. It isn't pretty."

When they got to Grotto Falls, Jolene stopped the train. Tater had obviously caught his scent and joined them. After a sniff all around, the animals adjusted to her presence.

Caleb was a bit baffled. "That's it. You just stop, and they stop? Monkey see monkey do?" He chuckled at Tater's antics and ruffled her ears.

"That's it." Jolene pulled out some mesh masks and showed Caleb how to pull them over the muzzles of the llamas.

"You afraid they'll munch their way to the top?"

She grinned. "Don't want them nibbling on mountain laurel or rhododendron. They're poisonous plants."

They went another mile or so, then rested near a stream, and the llamas bent their heads to drink.

Caleb looked surprised. "What about their masks? Shouldn't we remove them?"

"Only if you want extra work and to lose time. They suck — not lap, like dogs do."

Tater barked her agreement.

"This is a good stopping point. We'll give them a snack while we rest. As you know, the trail gets tougher once we get to Trillium Gap."

Caleb reckoned they were about a third of the way into their trek when he found out the other reason why he was placed at the rear of the train. Seemed the trail was also their poop collector. He decided to ask, "Is llama poop sumthin' we scoop and trek out?"

She laughed. "We should. Llama beans sell quite well."

"Lima beans?"

Jolene looked at him. "We call llama poop *beans*."

Caleb seemed confused. "Why? They look like Junior Mints or brown biscuits, not beans."

"Dunno. Why do people call bull balls mountain oysters? They just do. We're not picking them up, because they're rich in nutrients — good for the soil."

"Now I know why I got this end of the train."

"You smell anything?"

He sniffed. "Huh. I don't smell 'em."

"No shit!"

He chuckled. "I guess this is the first time shit don't stink."

She threw him a wry look. "I rest my case. Besides, the rear end isn't so bad."

Caleb checked out her rear and silently agreed.

The trail was quiet, except for the tree talk and bird song that whispered as they climbed. Sun slanted through the leafy canopy, highlighting a wildflower here a fern there.

After a few moments, Jolene broke the silence. "Actually, you may have something there. Llama manure is great for the environment and is an excellent fertilizer. Sells well. Hmmm . . ."

"I can't believe we're still talking about poop."

She winked. "Feel the line. See the rhythm? It conveys their mood. They must like you, because we're humming along just fine. Just be sure not to jiggle or bounce the line."

"Why?"

"Spooks them and causes llama drama."

They continued to climb steadily from there. Finally, they reached the last steep stretch and were at the lodge in no time. Arriving alongside the kitchen, Caleb helped hitched the llamas to the posts, and the entire lodge crew unloaded the unconventional packs and scurried away to stock the pantry. Jolene went inside to get the llamas their treats and came out with stacks of pancakes.

Caleb lifted his brow in surprise. "Pancakes? I know they're good, but . . ."

"Yup. The llamas get to munch on hotcakes for a job well done." She handed Beauty another flapjack.

Tim walked over and asked Caleb, "How'd it go?"

"Worked like a charm. Way easier and less smelly than I thought it would be. My vote's a yes."

"Well, I'll be durned," Jim said, slapping Caleb on the back. "Looks like we gonna git some llamas of our own. After y'all wash up and eat, we'll talk business."

Jolene beamed.

Caleb made a mental note. *Remember to get some bells to give the bears warning we're comin' round the mountain.*

# CHAPTER ELEVEN: OH, WHAT A FEELING

Caleb felt like a new man. There was extra pep in his step that hadn't been there for years, and it seemed to be connected to Jolene. She told him she had been temporarily assigned to LeConte Lodge for the season. He figured when his schedule permitted—usually after his time off—he could work it out to accompany her up with the train on their regular Monday morning runs.

It didn't take long before the llamas were packed up with dirty linens and trash, and he was heading out with Jolene on the downward trek. At the foot of the trail, the transport trailer was parked. They led the animals into the trailer, giving them a carrot to munch on for the ride back to the farm. Neither Caleb nor Jolene accompanied them, since their shift had ended. After Jolene turned down Frank's offer to drive her *home*, she asked Caleb for a ride to her temporary digs.

Jolene's company had housed her near the foot of the mountain at a nice cabin beside Mynatt Park.

"Make yourself at home. Shower's that away." She jerked her thumb toward the bathroom.

"Don't mind if I do." He turned the water on, adjusted it, then peeled off his clothes and jumped into the shower. *Nuthin' like a hot shower. Good for what ails ye.*

Suddenly, Jolene's voice snapped his attention.

"Mind if I join y'all?" In her hand, she flashed a small foil packet. "I hope you don't mind?"

Caleb's manhood hardened immediately. Despite fatigue and sweat from the hike, he was hot and ready. He stepped aside. "Be my guest." His response was instinctive and immediate.

Jolene joined him — in every sense of the word.

All the fantasies of sex he'd had while washing up at Rainbow Falls came true when he lifted her hips over his throbbing cock. *Reality is much better than fantasy.*

Afterward, she said, "I trust that was satisfactory?"

He looked at her as they dried each other off. "I'm not rightly sure." He wrapped himself in the plush towel. "Might need to conduct some more . . . finding out . . ."

Jolene pulled him by the towel to her bedroom. "How about we do sumthin' about that?" She pushed him onto the bed, freed him from his towel, knelt between his thighs, and took his rising rod into her mouth. When she was done, she asked, "How was that?"

"Umm very good. Thank you, ma'am. Shall I return the favor?"

Jolene rocked back on her heels. "If you insist. I'm no priss, prude, or pill."

He cocked a brow. "Hmm, that so? Y'all must be a pickle then. A sweet Gherkin, maybe?"

"Or a pepper."

He gave her a slow smile. "A chipotle or chili?"

"You tell me."

He gazed up at her after he brought her to another climax. "That was one red-hot pepper."

He cleaned up again — alone this time — then took the time to jot her a note asking her to meet him at The Pioneer Inn. He made it into a paper airplane and left the bathroom. "Incoming," he said as it made its way to her.

Laughing, she retrieved, unfolded, and read it. "This a date?"

"You want it to be?"

"I don't date. I'm into now, the present moment. No

strings, no rings, no vows."

He chuckled. "It's dinner. Not a marriage proposal."

"Good, because I'm not into commitments. I'm a tumbleweed. I go wherever I'm blown."

Caleb shook his head in denial. "Don't give me that. I don't think so. You go where you wanna go, do what you wanna do. So it's not a date. In fact, it's a non-date. Will I see you there?"

"Maybe." She winked.

Caleb climbed into his Ford and drove to the Sugarlands Lodge. *Thank God, ain't no hikin' involved here.* While there was no road to LeConte Lodge — just five trails — there was a quite nice road to the Lodge at Elkmont. The Lodge required no trails to hike, no helicopters, and no llamas to get there.

When Caleb reached the Lodge, he avoided the kitchen entrance and went to the front reception area. *Ain't like I'm dodgin' Millie none. Just wanna make a proper entrance.*

Pat was in the small office, while Emma Jean had earned her place at the registration desk. She got the usually pleasant task of welcoming guests.

Her short black hair was streaked with platinum, and she looked almost regal but approachable and adorable. She was talking to some dude. Interrupting them didn't seem wrong.

Caleb swooped his aunt up in a swinging hug, laughing. "Hey, Auntie Em, how you doin'?"

She returned the laugh and pecked him on the cheek. "Set me down, boy! Plumb near gave me a heart attack."

He winked. "Not me. More likely that ole dude who's checkin' y'all out."

Emma Jean made sweeping motions. "Shoo. Off with ye. That'll be the day."

But Caleb caught the flush rise in her cheeks as the gentleman stood aside. She stole a glance at another distinguished-looking guest who was dressed in black from head to toe.

She turned back to him. "Stayin' the weekend, Caleb? In for the Annual Fiddle Fest?"

"Yep, wouldn't miss it. It be tomorrow night, right?"

Emma Jean nodded. "This man here is Mister O'Toole. He's joinin' in the competition."

"That so?" Caleb leaned back on his heels, sizing the man up. He approached to take a closer look. The man wore a worn cowboy hat and boots embossed with white cactus flowers, looking familiar. "Y'all be Wailin' Wally?"

The man tipped his hat and drawled, "That'd be a yes."

Caleb sucked in a breath and let it out slowly. "Well, I'll be durned. Y'all excel at guitar. Am I right?"

Wally nodded.

Caleb's eyes sharpened. "Y'all aimin' to compete in the *fiddle* show? Thought ye only played the guitar."

The man nodded again. "That I am. I play a mean fiddle, too." Wally tipped his hat. "Ma'am, if y'all excuse me . . ." he said as he walked away.

Caleb got the message. "I'll be seein' y'all, then."

A teasing light was present in Emma Jean's gaze. "Y'all worried, Caleb?"

"Nope. I learned at Uncle Lem's knee, and he won every contest ever held. Ah aim to do likewise."

She chuckled. "I'll see ye later. You eatin' here?"

Caleb shook his head. "Think I'll eat out."

Emma Jean added, "Don't need to worry about Millie. She's not on duty tonight."

"No matter. I'm goin' to The Pioneer Inn. Got a non-date." *At least I hope I do.*

Emma Jean's eyebrows lifted in surprise. "That's a new one on me. A non-date?"

"Yep. I gotta tumbleweed girl." He grinned and winked. "Hard to pin down."

Emma Jean wagged her finger at him. "When someone tells ye who they are, believe 'em."

Caleb went to the family quarters, flexed his fingers, and picked up his fiddle. He applied green rosin to the bow hair and went out on the veranda to serenade Blanket Mountain in the distance. Soon guests — drawn no doubt by the music — were tapping their toes and singing along. He spied Wally O'Toole out of the corner of his eye, his fiddle case in hand. *Is he goin' somewhere to practice? Don't matter much. I'm aimin' to win.*

Then he addressed the small gathering as he put his fiddle in its case. "See y'all tomorrow night at the Fiddle Fest." He went back inside and cleaned up for his non-date.

The Pioneer Inn was an authentic mountain cabin upgraded into a restaurant popular with the locals. It sat at the beginning of a strip of shops and was one of the few with free and easy parking. He entered and was led through the inside. The server stopped when they reached the patio overlooking the river. The water roared over its rock-filled stretch near the table he was given.

He knew better than to order for his commitment-phobic non-date, provided Jolene showed up. In the olden days, men often ordered for their dates. That she-devil would beat his ass should he be so condescending.

Caleb ordered a beer and watched the river bounce the wild ducks as it cascaded over several rocks. After a bit, the sun dipped low, and the light changed. He was in the process of deciding whether to place his own order or wait when the shiny auburn head bent next to his.

Jolene's warm breath teased his ear. "This seat taken?"

"It is now." He got up to move the chair as she slid her fit body into the ladder-backed chair.

"Whatcha up to?"

"Nuthin'. Just fiddlin' around some."

She gave him a slow smile. "Are you suggesting you wanna fiddle with me?"

He leaned forward, grinning. "Only if you plan to sing along."

When the wait staffer arrived, Jolene ordered a *Bud Light*. "What makes you think I can sing?"

He cocked a brow. Then waggled both. "If memory serves, I heard y'all singin' in the shower this very afternoon. Would you care to repeat the performance?"

She winked. "Maybe."

Caleb enjoyed his mountain trout and appreciated the moans of dining delight that issued from Jolene. Lingering over coffee, he was surprised when the tall form he recognized approached the far end of the patio, where a microphone stand and stool stood. Soon the mellow tones of the Tennessee Waltz caught everyone's ear. The fiddler was none other than the famous Wailin' Wally.

Wally needed no introduction. He began to play a rousing *Cattle in the Corn* next. People were on their feet by the time he finished his rendition. Then he played *Turkey in the Straw* and laid his fiddle aside when the song ended.

Wally addressed the diners. "Thank ye, thank ye. But I'm not the only fiddler enjoying this mighty fine establishment." With a nod and using his bow, he pointed to Caleb. "How 'bout it, Caleb?"

Caleb nodded but showed his empty hands, indicating he had no fiddle with him. He shrugged.

Not to let it rest, Wally extended his own fiddle to Caleb. There were no two ways about it. Caleb had no excuse.

He took the famed fiddle and made a slight bow. "Mighty obliged. This is an honor." Caleb took the fiddle and bow and played *My Tennessee Home*. The swooping melody soared through the air. He played only one song, then tipped his head to Wally and the crowd and escorted Jolene out.

Jolene looked pleased. "You're a real interesting dude. What else don't I know about you?"

As he drove her home, he replied, "Maybe y'all'll get lucky, and I'll show you."

There was a hot time in Jolene's cabin that night when Caleb showed Jolene what else he could do.

The next day, a fire burned inside Caleb, and he planned to fan the flames whenever he could. He had a bounce to his step and a light in his eyes he hadn't seen in a long while. The outstanding sex was just a part of it. There was just something intoxicating about Jolene.

He spent the morning soaking in the peace of the mountains. He thought he loved them because they were beautiful, a balm creating calm, making music in his heart, and poetry in his soul. Unlike the unrest of his life, the mountains were ever-present. Constant. There, the same, no matter what else was happening. But he was wrong.

In reality, the mountains were ever-changing. The view varied by the slant of sunshine, the shadow of a cloud, changing seasons, the ethereal mists, even the movement of birds and animals. Thinking deeply, Caleb determined that anything ever-present and ever-changing at the same time was worth seeing. An artist could only hope to capture the briefest of moments. It was never the same, ever. If you blinked, you'd miss something.

In short, the mountain diversity was the very thing that engaged him thoroughly and completely. He let their dynamic magic act like an elixir to prepare him for the fiddle contest that night. He felt excitement bubbling in his chest until his fingers itched to play. He flexed them and let the anticipation build and fill him.

The evening at the Gatlinburg Convention Center was hopping. Visitors from across the nation were competing. It was a large venue, and folks from the surrounding area packed the place. Over fifty participants were slated to play. Blue Grass and Country Music dominated the theme with several sets planned, arranged by instrument. Banjo, guitar, mandolin, and fiddle matches commanded the largest audience.

Contestants of the Fiddle Fest were judged on the style, rhythm, and tone of their music. Each repertoire had to consist of three musical categories, hoedown, waltz, and one of their choice. Each song had to be played within a maximum of six minutes. Caleb's strategy was not to select new songs for the fest but to choose his best.

Fiddlers delighted the audience with their humor and hollerin'. Some yelled, letting the fiddle swell with rhythm. Others even yodeled. One contestant reported the winner in his set had out-hollered him, not out-played him.

Caleb used his natural charm with the audience, and his good looks didn't hurt none either, but he did not rely on gimmicks. He let the notes flow through him, becoming one with the instrument. He was merely the vessel through which the melody poured. He was pumped, more than ready. *Thanks, Jolene. Last night was wicked good.*

He played as he was born to play. He wasn't nervous or worried, he just played from his heart. Nothing on earth satisfied him quite like fiddlin'. Women had claimed they felt their heart lift straight out of their chests — just a little — until the song ended and it returned to their heaving breasts.

Some of the fiddlers stood up while others sat down while playing. Some tipped their chair over in their frenzy. Others played sad songs. Or gospel songs. Or patriotic songs. All sorts shook the rafters. Serious ones. Silly ones. But no one could play them quite like Caleb. He played exquisitely plaintive melodies, rousing waltzes, and stomp-your-feet songs. He made granny women laugh and young ones sigh. His playing kept old folks from drowsing and young men's blood coursing. He planned to do no less tonight.

Wally went on and performed as expected. He was not a

showboat, but he did have undeniable style. The crowd ate it up, digested it, and went wild. Everyone loved it and him. Caleb overheard some people claiming Wally made them forget who they were and where they lived.

Caleb had to follow him in the lineup. He set his spanky-twang loose when it was his turn. He began the set with the classic old-time favorite, *Turkey in the Straw*. But as he played his second song, he had to abandon his bow midway when the tip popped off and the hairs went flying.

That didn't force Caleb to stop playing. He simply changed the position of the fiddle from his chest to his chin and began to play with both hands — the pizzicato method Uncle Lem had drilled into him. He heard those close to the stage claiming the strings smoked. He fiddled like never before. When he performed his last song, he added his harmonica to its holder and played both. No one had ever played faster. Not angels. Not devils. Everyone was on their feet.

After Caleb completed his set, Wally slapped him on the back. The man claimed he'd lay money on Caleb's ability to play a bud into bloom only so it could dance along to his tune.

The contest between Caleb and Wally was so close, the judges decided the winner would be determined by playing *The Devil Went Down to Georgia*. They would be performing together in what was dubbed *the Dueling Devils*. Caleb poured his heart and soul into dueling with Wally on stage.

The crowd went wild as Caleb and Wally bowed and twisted and upped the tempo, then raised that even higher. They played their best until, at the same moment, they stopped, laughing and back-slapping each other. Wally took off his hat and fanned Caleb. Caleb tipped his hat and did the same to Wally. They kept on fanning until the crowd went quiet to hear the judges' decision.

In the end, they were both awarded the championship. It was *not* declared a tie. Both men took home the top prize money, and another trophy would be ordered, so each had one to display.

Emma Jean jumped to her feet with the rest of the crowd. She'd seen Caleb play the circuit for years but never like he played this night. *Whoever his mystery woman is, she's sweetened his soul and healed his heart.* She was glad to see it. *His lot in life hasn't been easy. Surviving the loss of love, whether it be a parent or a woman, still stings. He's learned to live with his losses but seeing him now does my heart good.*

Emma Jean had noticed Millie and Herman and their children among the crowd. The children had danced along with Millie while Herman stood, slapping his knees in time with Caleb's flying fingers.

Emma Jean and Pat joined Millie and her family as they left the Convention Center.

Millie was flushed like the rest of the audience. "That music man! No one can play like Caleb. Sometimes I swear I catch a riff from his harmonica a-sailin' in the breeze. I always feel lighter when I hear it."

Emma Jean nodded. *Is there a remnant of feelings for Caleb in Millie's soul? For both their sakes, I hope not.* "I've heard it too. That's Caleb talkin' to the trees."

But it was an auburn-haired woman who seemed to catch Caleb's eye, if she wasn't mistaken. Perhaps he played to her now. Maybe she was the one who put the sparkle back in his eyes.

Caleb was drenched in sweat, but the smile stretched across his face was something he hadn't felt in twenty years. Some fan handed him a cold one, and if there was a lawman in the audience, none objected. He gulped it down.

The swarming crowd surrounded him, pressing on his

soaked shirt. He undid the buttons attempting to cool down while he scanned the mob of people. He saw Aunt Emma Jean and Pat in the crowd and swore he spotted Jolene, too. Pushed along by the surging throng toward the exit, he couldn't muster the energy to pursue Jolene. He decided to just head home to the Lodge.

That night he slept like a log.

He rested on Sunday with a short hike to let the hills restore him. After all, he had a mountain to climb come Monday. This time he decided to pack his fiddle for his return to LeConte Lodge.

Caleb geared up to face Millie the next morning but was met by a much younger version of her. Caleb jolted at her resemblance to Millie.

The lass took his order. "Hey, Mister 'Leb, whatcha eatin' this morning?"

He reckoned this twin was Emmie Jo. "That you, Miss Lady Jane? Lady Isadora with y'all? What y'all doin' here all growed up and all?"

"Not sure where my sister is, but I'm workin' for Ma. She's breakin' me in. Started me off bussing tables as soon as I turned old enough. Now, I'm up to waitressin', done with dish washin'." She wrinkled her nose. "I wanna cook. She knows I can."

"Seems like just yesterday, I was teachin' y'all to fish."

The young woman grinned. "She just don't want the competition, I reckon."

Caleb winked. *More like Millie knows the way to a man's heart is way south of his stomach, and she don't want her young'un findin' that out quite yet.*

Emmie Jo smiled, took his order, and grabbed another mug to pour Emma Jean some brew as she pulled out a chair to join Caleb.

"Make that a double order," he said. "My guess is Auntie

Em hasn't eaten either."

Emma Jean laughed, nodded, then smothered a yawn with her hand. "I was out late last night. Lawd, y'all shoulda seen the commotion after y'all left the other night. Folks are still talkin' about the Fiddle Fest."

Caleb smiled. "Gonna take my fiddle back with me this time. Folks up there are likin' my harmonica, but I miss the feel of the strings."

Emma Jean nodded. "Sounds like you found your niche, but I wager somethin' else has put that light in your eyes. Who is she?"

"What makes you think there's a woman involved?"

"There always is. Nothing else puts that gleam in a man's eye."

Caleb winked.

The slam of the old screen door alerted them to Millie's arrival. She removed the coffee pot from her daughter, shooing her away, and bent to top off his coffee. "Congratulations, Mr. Champion. You outdid yourself. Always said you was a music man. I heard you been playin' in festivals all over the place."

He smiled, and for the first time, didn't bat an eye over Millie's presence. "Y'all heard right. I been showing up in states I never expected to see." In fact, he'd been quite tight-lipped about it, but every few months, he'd disappear, playing in competitions hither and yon.

# CHAPTER TWELVE: TIME AFTER TIME

Caleb woke with Jolene to the cool morning before the sun rose. They were up before daybreak getting the llamas set for the trek. He felt like an old hand, and he and Jolene functioned well together. He had mastered the routine and looked forward to the trip up his favorite mountain.

Caleb loaded the panniers on some of the animals. The llamas hummed as they stood waiting to be loaded for the upward trek. They blew air through their nostrils like horses and suddenly made a very unhorse-like screech. Usually, the sounds they made reminded him of the Wookie in Star Wars, but this sound was higher in pitch.

Caleb wondered if they picked up the scent of a bear or boar. Was that what they were trying to tell him? He hoped not. He couldn't begin to imagine the chaos should they, once outfitted and lined up, encounter an unfamiliar animal out of nowhere. Would they stop? Bunch up? That wouldn't be good. Wouldn't the lines tangle? He shuddered at the thought.

Jolene appeared happy and unconcerned, though. She waggled her eyebrows at him. "The other night was far out. Only one thing missing . . ."

He raised a brow. "Oh? What?"

"The nookie afterward."

He guffawed. "We can make up for that."

She winked. "Count on it."

He copped a feel of her firm breast and swatted her mighty fine ass as he led a loaded llama past her. When they stopped along the trail for a break, Caleb approached her. "Ready for that quickie?"

In a split second, Jolene undid her jeans, and the next thing Caleb knew, she was all over him. He lifted her onto his instantly hard rod, impaling her much like his ever-present fantasies of Rainbow Falls, only without the icy spray.

After they reached the lodge, unloaded the llamas, and ate lunch, Caleb helped reload the animals with garbage and laundry for the trip down. He wasn't scheduled for the downward run and wouldn't see Jolene again until Wednesday. He was very glad they'd got it on when they did.

The sex they had gave him energy, and later that night at Cliff Top, he played his fiddle for the crowd. Too bad Jolene wasn't there. He could have used the afterward nookie she'd talked about. When the glorious sunset leaked from the sky, he played his newest tune. It appeared to be the perfect end to his set and the day.

Bo had a field day with that, teasing him unmercifully, but Caleb paid him no mind.

Caleb and Jolene had spent most of the nineties following the same schedule and making love whenever possible. The relationship had worked well like that, and they were both comfortable with it.

For the first several years, Caleb had worked the spring through fall season. When he'd felt renewed and restored enough to spend some time alone, he'd taken on the winter caretaker job on a trial basis. He'd spent his first winter with general upkeep, snow removal, and the usual odd jobs that arose. He fell into a happy routine of working the lodge during the season and enjoying the solitude of the winter months atop LeConte.

During the lodge's open season, when he wasn't taking

care of guests or leading the llama train with Jolene, he'd fiddle to entertain the crew and guests. He'd often include some of his famous storytelling. While the others limited themselves to sharing ghost stories, Caleb preferred telling his *Granny Women* stories. He had several within his repertoire, ranging from growling old apple trees with howling apples to commitment-phobe bachelors intent on avoiding marriage. He'd occasionally throw in one of his favorite Wiley Oakley stories just to keep his memory alive.

In the isolation of the winter months, Caleb's leisure time was spent reading, playing his fiddle for the mountains, or merely contemplating the ever-changing conditions of the summit. Sometimes a hoar frost covered the landscape and the trees, creating a mystical wonderland. Other times the tree branches were coated by snow, bowing down with its weight. He enjoyed the tree talk too. It whispered sometimes, or whistled, roared, crooned, sang, whooshed, moaned, groaned, and soared. There was a symphony of natural sounds worth the time it took to listen.

Some mornings a freezing fog socked him in and swallowed the view, but he loved it all. Of course, there were the occasions when hot memories of Jolene forced him outdoors for a brisk short hike, regardless of the conditions. He did avoid Cliff Top when the ground was too icy, because to slip there could bring sudden death. There were also peaceful times when he would simply succumb to the solitude and sleep the day away.

Life at the top of Mount LeConte meant no intrusive politics or troubling news of the day that permeated the news waves. With no television or electricity, the only thing he missed during the winter was the lively banter with Jolene, her direct, cryptic perspective, and her hot, firm body. There were days when he literally itched for her touch, making him toss and turn beneath his Hudson Bay blankets.

In Caleb's opinion, missing Jolene was one thousand times better than being insane with pain over Millie and Herman. Although he was glad to have escaped the mania of the advent of the new millennium and the scare of the Y2K, he'd have preferred to ring in the new century with Jolene. There was no chance of that, though. It wasn't safe to climb the trails to LeConte Lodge during the winter, and Jolene wasn't dumb enough to even try.

Spring 2003

The onset of springtime on LeConte reveals itself subtly — a tender green shoot here, the promise of a trillium there. The temperatures rise from bitter cold to the balmy forties. That was when Caleb would make good use of the washbasin and soap. He'd also make sure to shave his winter beard away. The helicopters dropped off supplies for the new season in March, and when the frost left the mountain, the llamas and their wranglers started their treks, and life at the lodge got back to normal.

Over the years, Caleb's reunions with Jolene had become almost legend with the regular crew of the lodge. After lunch was over, the crew knew the routine and would scatter, and he and Jolene would head to his cabin and not emerge for hours.

With each year, Caleb's relationship with Jolene flowered into something quite close to love. However, he had no plans to jump into love again. *No way, no how, nuh-uh.* His battle-worn bruised heart was barely intact, and he planned to keep it that way.

Caleb yearned and burned for Jolene over the winter month. Yet deep down, he knew she was like the dandelion seeds, blowing easily onward and away, so he generally made no demands.

However, when the new season rolled around, he was determined to make his case. He wanted more.

He planned to urge Jolene to try wintering with him at the LeConte Lodge. There was something so satisfying about staying there for a long spell. Something that soothed the soul and calmed the relentless restlessness. He wanted to share that with her like he shared his body and their many passionate, hot encounters.

As the season rolled on, Jolene began to lengthen her stays by training additional staff to spell her so she could spend more time with Caleb. She would join him, the crew, and the guests not only on day hikes but also in the evenings when he charmed his audience with tales of the trails he'd roamed. He would often break into song, playing favorites on his fiddle or harmonica. Jolene's dulcet tones rounded out the evening when she joined him singing ballads and loves songs. He always ended their evenings wrapping his arms around Jolene with either rousing or gentle lovemaking in mind, much to the chagrin of the female guests who volleyed for his attention.

Yet, though the season had started off with their usual hot reunion, there seemed to be an edge to it this time. Caleb had begun to feel something coming on stealthily but steadily the last several seasons but had put it out of his mind. Their treks up and down the mountain were not quite as complacent or peaceful as they had been for years. More and more, he, well, he wanted more. More something.

"Winter here with me." He'd repeated variations on that theme throughout the season. But winter was approaching, and he wanted her answer.

She laughed it off as she did most times. "You don't want me around full time. Trust me."

"But I do. We fit together like two olives on a swizzle stick in one of them fancy-dancy James Bond flicks."

Jolene moved closer until she was upfront and personal. She put her finger on his lips to shush him, then pinched his butt and shook her head, declining gently but firmly.

"Try it, you might like it. Stay with me."

She laughed and shrugged. "Things are fine the way they are. I'm a senior wrangler with pension and benefits. Every year some young buck tries to make inroads into my standing. Few women ever get as high in the Outfitters. I'm fortunate they still let me wrangle."

No longer a young buck, Caleb peered over the half-glasses he sometimes wore. "What are you going to do when you're sixty?"

She slanted a smile in his direction and winked. "Same thing you plan to do. Think about it when I'm fifty-nine."

He tried to lighten up. "I'm not asking you to be my cutie patootie or anything."

"I should hope not — whatever that is."

He grinned and nuzzled her neck. He felt her shivers. He aimed to create more with well-placed brushes of hot breath grazing her face and ear. He led her by the hand — ignoring her protest — to the grove they'd found at Myrtle Point and dubbed their lovemaking nest. Using his feet, he scrunched the dry soft pine needles into an organic mattress.

He knelt down, pulling her with him.

She trembled in his arms.

"Think of the sex we'd be in for, the music we could make in and out of bed. Indoors" — he bit her neck in little nips — "and out." The tree breeze had a touch of cold to it, whispering a warning. A warning he ignored.

Jolene laughed this time but didn't swat him away. She turned fully into him, and they began slowly peeling the clothes from their bodies to create the music that climaxing in the freedom of the outdoors made possible. Her rendition beat the chorus of the katydids under the full moon on a hot summer night.

When they were through—bathed and warmed—enjoying their afterglow, he tried again. "Not asking for a lifetime here, Jolene. Just a winter. Of mellow music and loads of snugglin', kissin', lovin' to our heart's content."

She raised a brow. "Or it could be a winter of our discontent."

"Not likely."

She sat up fumbling with her clothes, pulling them on fast. "My IRA is compounding. I don't want to—"

He sat up fast and pulled his flannel shirt over his head to settle on his shoulders. "There it is. You *don't want to.*"

"Well, I don't. Why can't you just drop it?" Her tone was dry and flat.

His frustration burst into a raised voice. "Why don't you just *try* it? Oh, that's right. You don't want to." He stood and stalked away, hearing the sound of her breath exploding from her lungs in his wake.

Then she yelled, "I have a final run down the mountain to prepare for. I don't have time for this. This is what I'm talking about. We'd get on each other's nerves."

He stormed off. *You knew this day would come, Caleb. Carry on. Forget about it. Fool. Shame on me.* He stomped down the trail, unhappy and angry.

The coldness he'd heard in her voice rivaled the increasing chill in the air.

When she caught up to him, he grumbled, "The weather's changin'. Maybe you should leave tomorrow instead of waiting until the last run. Let me check the weather report."

"Fiddlesticks. I already did. What's the fuss? This light dusting of snow is better than hiking in the rain. Besides, snow this time of year is more novel than nuisance. The llamas don't mind it."

He shook his head. "Mountain weather is unpredictable.

Unlike yourself. Full steam ahead. Your way or the highway."

She feigned a move, swiping her hands. "Back off. Complaints, Complaints. Stop. Your praise going to my head."

He threw her a wry grin and shook his head. "Woman, sometimes dealing with you is like hugging a porcupine."

"So? I'll kiss it and make it all better then." She quipped.

"Prick me is more likely."

When the llama train was packed with its last load for the season, Jolene sought him out and gave him a kiss. "While I'm gone, maybe y'all ought to think on this. When a gal tells ye what's what, believe her or leave her."

He gaped at her in surprise. "Say what?"

She winked. "Just a word to the wise. See ye when I see ye."

*Guess our last time lovin' was just for auld lang syne.* Caleb sighed. He heard the llama bells fade as they made their way down the steep slope. There had been ice in her tone, but worse, there was actually ice in the wind.

"Take care," he whispered to the wind.

And she was gone.

# CHAPTER THIRTEEN: SHE'S NOT THERE

November 2003

After the llama train left, Caleb had had enough drama for the day. He walked back to the kitchen and poured himself a cuppa joe, wishing it was moonshine instead.

There was a bite to the wind. Light rain fell from the gray clouds that moved in suddenly. This was too early in the season for bad weather. No weather forecast included more than a slight possibility of snow flurries to the north. It was only November.

He usually didn't even see snow by Christmas, but the weather had definitely been changing for the worse the last few years. *I'm not worried. The crew knows how to handle changing conditions.*

Still, worry uncoiled and snaked through his thoughts. *The crew will be okay. They are all experienced hikers. Not concerned. Not pessimistic. No, not me. Jolene's fine, too. She knows what she's doing. Nothing to fret about. What I am concerned about, though, is Bo's leading the llama train. Is he capable of dealing with the llamas in this weather? He's Jolene's last line of defense. Wait . . . Frank's with them, so they'll be okay.*

Jolene and the summer season crew began the steep descent. Bo was ahead of her, leading the llamas. She brought up the rear because she'd had to make her goodbyes with Caleb. Their send-off was not like the other times. They usually parted on much better terms. She wasn't used to feeling so churned up. *I warned him from the beginning. I'm not patootie material or whatever he's talking about.* She preferred her freedom — liked to go where she wanted when she wanted — and their parting upset her inner equilibrium. She was feeling off-center, and she didn't like it. *Not one little bit.*

The sun was blocked by gray-white low-lying clouds that stretched forever, making it overcast and difficult to see clearly. It was cold and getting colder by the moment. The rain turned into minuscule ice pellets, With the wind whipping them into stinging projectiles.

The cold permeated Jolene's bones, making her joints throb with her efforts to hike onward. *Should we turn back?* Jolene tried to catch Frank's attention, but the wind blew her words away. Ahead of her, Bo struggled with the line. *He better not bounce the line.* The wind's howls were too loud for the range of her cries. She watched her foggy breath flying in the opposite direction. She struggled to tug her glove on, holding the line with one hand. Fumbling with the glove, she jerked the line and had to reach out to rebalance the panniers.

The llamas suddenly shifted in their lines and got restless as a result. *Why? My clumsiness? A bear? The barometric pressure? What?* Something was apparently off for them, too. In general, llamas performed their best in cold temperatures, but storms, not so much — storms spooked them. Was one approaching? The weather service hadn't mentioned anything about a possible storm.

A light but steady mix of rain, ice, and snow started falling, coating the roots and rock along the trail. The granular slush made the narrow pathway slippery. They had reached the steepest grade on the slope when Lass, the second llama in the line, flat out stopped. The other llamas did not, plowing into each other and bunching up. A cascading mess of animals, lines, and humans followed. The unbalanced weight of the saddlebags caused the animals to stumble, further complicating matters. The rope jerked out of Jolene's grip. She saw Bo lose it as well. *What's happening?* The wind whipped through the trees as snow-heavy ice-coated branches dropped around her. *I wish Snow White and Snow Balls were here. They are more experienced llamas. Too late for that now. Should have heaved the panniers when I had the chance. Shit!*

Lady stumbled over Lass, further disrupting the train like tumbling dominoes. The panicked animals slid and tripped. Bess lurched into Jolene, and she lost her footing. Both she and Bess sailed over the edge, rolling on the slick slope, with pine needles, leaves, and small stones joining their fall. Jolene plummeted down the side of the cliff, arms and legs flailing. She screamed, and so did the llama. She was dazed, disoriented, and dizzy and then felt her head slam into something hard. In the distance, she heard the voices of her crew. The biting cold chilled her. Then blackness enveloped her.

After a staggering struggle, the crew straightened out and limped through the rapidly accumulating snow. Frank found himself battling to haul the llama pack back on their feet. He had to keep it together and get the team down the hill. He directed the crew to remove the saddlebags. They struggled to get them off, abandoning them where they lay. When he counted noses, two were missing, Jolene and Bess.

The wind whipped the biting snow across the creases in Frank's face, blowing his scarf into his eyes. He swiped it away but still couldn't see through the nearly white-out conditions. There was no way to go back and look for them. Who knew where Jolene and Bess were, or for that matter, where in hell they were? Well over two feet of snow rested on the path, which now was icy and heavy. The winds blew strongly, and the temperatures plunged.

The snow piled against the mountainside, creating deep

drifts. They had to tread carefully, plunging one foot deep before pulling the other up to step down again, rinse and repeat. Some llamas tried to lie down and quit, but Frank kept them going, and they finally made it down the mountain. Frank, with Lass and Lady in tow, reached the parking lot first. The rest of the crew and llamas straggled in behind them.

The truck and trailer were buried in deep snow, making driving home impossible. No way could they dig out. They had neither the shovels nor the energy to do it.

Unfortunately, one llama and one lone woman weren't among the stragglers.

Frank ordered the crew to put the llamas into the trailer — *thank God it's mostly enclosed* — and insisted that everyone bunker down within the transport as well. They covered every animal with their blankets, burrowing in with them, sharing the compartment. The combined body heat created the much-needed additional warmth and safety for humans and animals alike. The Storm of the Century continued to rage outside, dumping even more snow.

Frank and the crew lived on MREs, meals ready to eat in seconds, included as part of their standard packing practice. Luckily, they always kept extras stored in the trailer. That and the alfalfa cubes for the llamas would hopefully get them through the storm.

The wind moaned, and the snow-laden trees groaned in protest around them. It sounded like the misery of hell had been unloosed on earth, scaring the crap out of all of them.

The weather didn't break for six solid days. When help finally reached them, Frank learned the full extent of the storm's effect. The GSMNP had been virtually snowed in. It had taken days to get snow-removable equipment into the Park and even more time to clear the first section, from Cades Cove to Townsend. Mount LeConte hadn't even been a factor in the equation at the beginning. For a long time, it had been difficult to even get in some areas nearby the surrounding towns, let alone the backcountry.

Usually, the sun did some damage to the snowfall, but this snowpack was different. Everything about the winter was. The tangible evidence of climate change couldn't be denied. Temperatures had gotten as low as ten below zero on top of Mount LeConte. Far below in Gatlinburg, the temperature had dipped to one degree, which was unheard of. While usually much colder than the lower elevations, temperatures never dropped that low on Mount LeConte.

Frank notified whoever he could that Jolene was missing but was told it could be a long time before anyone could do much about her disappearance. Rangers were not immediately available, so he figured they must have been deployed for other tasks. He felt frustrated that there was nothing he could do to help Jolene.

It took until December just to clear two miles into town from the Sugarlands Visitors Center. The terrain around there was easy and flat but the Gatlinburg entrance to the National Park remained blocked. There were no phone lines to use and no one available to talk to until the snow was cleared and trucked out. The Park crew and officials were too busy digging out and handling the results of the storm.


Caleb's worry about Jolene and the llama train was not unfounded. LeConte Lodge itself lay buried beneath four feet of unprecedented snow. They got snow up at the summit, all right, but not like what he was seeing, and not so early in the year. *Thank God I have extra propane. And back up wood for the fireplace should it come down to that.*

Still, Caleb wondered how Bo and the rest of the crew had managed on the trek down. *The whole crew's together. They'll be fine.* But the wind whipping through the leafless boughs and whistling through the pines had him unsettled. *Jolene's tough.*

*Maybe even too tough. Independent. She hates relying on anyone most of the time.* Caleb knew one thing for sure. *If ye had to beg a person to stay in your life, that one didn't belong there.* He'd come as close to that as anyone. He did have his pride. After all was said and done, he hadn't asked her to become his bride. All he'd proposed was to be at his side *one* winter.

Caleb reminded himself that she had dressed well for the trip. She'd worn her *GORE-TEX* jacket, her alpine flap hat, and *IsoDry* wear, and her boots were broken in. *She should be fine as wine. I'm frettin' like a turkey scratchin' the ground lookin' fer grub. Why am I fussin'?* But he knew. He was upset. He cared far more than he let on. It felt suspiciously like love. *That's a fine kettle of fish. Lovin' a tumbleweed. Crazy, I must be losing' it. She ain't lookin' to be tied down. Doubt she'll ever be ready for that. Over and out. She came right out and told me so. Hell, man, read the effin' writin' on the wall.* He sighed and shook his head.

March 2004

Frank led the llama team up to the LeConte Lodge for the first run of the new season. While he had heard that the NPS, National Guard, and even the military had used helicopters for rescue missions during and after the storm, Jolene had not been found among the rescued.

Newspaper stories from across the nation had reported on the drama at the time. None had included anything about LeConte Lodge. Not when stranded hikers, tourists, and eighty students from an affluent northern private college-prep school were taking center stage. One lost woman hadn't factored into any news report.

It didn't help that Jolene had no family calling in to see if she was okay, unlike the other hikers. It was as if Jolene had dropped off the face of the earth, and nobody cared.

When Frank had reminded officials that Jolene was still missing, they feared she was either buried in the snow or had wandered outside the Park. They had alerted personnel in neighboring parks, but nothing and no one surfaced. Frank sure hoped he wouldn't find her body on their current trek.

When they reached the area where Jolene had gone missing, Frank and the team searched high and low for any sign of her. They found the body of Bess on a ledge far below, but there was no reason to endanger themselves to recover her. Even the panniers were out of reach.

As they made their way, the wranglers and new season's crew had taken care to gather what they could of the other panniers, but even that yielded precious little. Bits of bed-linens packed down from the lodge for laundering were seen scattered hither and yon—not all of it was possible to gather.

Troubled thoughts pestered Frank with their persistence as they approached the lodge. *How am I going to tell Caleb? He'll have no idea. No way of knowing Jolene is missing.* He had to tell Caleb, or the others would. *After all, everyone on this trek had their eyes peeled, looking for Jolene—even if they did not want to find her body.*

Caleb had used his small battery-powered radio to listen to the weather stations talk about what they called *The Storm of the Century.* He'd heard that 26 states had been reporting record low temperatures and record high snowfalls. Even the Florida panhandle recorded half a foot of snow. He hadn't heard much about Mount LeConte, but all he'd had to do was take a gander through a window.

Caleb worried throughout the winter about the fate of those on the last trip of the season—especially Jolene. When he signed up for wintering at LeConte Lodge, he'd known there was no way anyone could safely risk the treacherous trails once it closed for the season. When the last crew members had left with the llamas, it was just him until springtime came again. If the blizzard had taught them anything, it was not to risk hiking in the winter when the weather could and did turn on a dime.

The arrival of the annual supply helicopters kept Caleb and some early crew busy unloading supplies, inventorying, and storing them. They were expecting the first llama train of the season in the afternoon. It was going to be a busy day.

Caleb hoped Jolene had mellowed over their winter apart, and she'd be the gal he cared about. However, when the llamas arrived, he didn't see Jolene in the lead. *Maybe she's at the rear.*

He swallowed his disappointment but wondered why the wranglers seemed more subdued than usual. By the time the first llama was tied to the hitching post, he finally realized Jolene wasn't among them at all. He figured she'd taken another job to stay away from him. Their parting had been strained, and she had made her position clear. Not to mention that he had been right about the weather, and Jolene hated being wrong and never conceded when she was.

He had harbored doubts that she'd return after their last goodbye. Still, he'd hoped time would have settled her down, and they'd pick up where they left off like they usually did. *Maybe she just took this summer off . . .*

He helped unload the pack llamas but couldn't help when his gaze repeatedly strayed to the mouth of the trail. *Maybe she's just laggin', getting ready to launch some prank on me.* After all, she had a wicked sense of humor.

But when Frank, hat in his hands, fingering its brim, stood in front of him awkwardly after rushing the others away, Caleb knew. He just knew, and his flicker of hope died. Jolene wasn't coming back. He'd played and replayed their last conversation. At least a million times, almost on a continuous loop. Had it been a tape like in the old days, it'd have worn out and broken.

*Where is she now?*

He raised a hand to shade his eyes from the glare of the sun and peered closely at Frank. "Somethin' on yer mind, Frank?"

Frank sighed and gestured toward the Dining Hall. He withdrew a flask from his hip pocket and poured some in two mugs. "Last trip down, there was an accident . . ."

Dread filled Caleb's belly like a coiled snake. He could hear his blood rushing in his ears, distorting Frank's words. Hesitant words he only heard intermittently.

"Storm of the Century . . . blizzard . . . four feet of snow . . . llama drama . . . Jolene disappeared . . ." Then Frank became clear as day. "We jist found Bess's body fifty feet down on the way up here — midway thru the switchback. Figured we'd let nature take its course. No way could we retrieve the animal . . ."

Caleb felt the blood leach from his face. The snake uncoiled and crawled up his spine, and a roar filled his ears. He gulped his drink and strode off in a haze. He shoved his hands in his pockets, his proud shoulders hunch and his head bent low as Frank's words echoed in his ears.

Frank shouted at his retreating back. "I'm tellin' ya, Caleb, there was nuthin' we could do . . . no trace of Jolene. I'm sorry, man."

# CHAPTER FOURTEEN: AIN'T NO MOUNTAIN HIGH ENOUGH

Summer 2004

From that point on, Caleb used every spare moment combing the hills, searching endlessly throughout the seasons where travel was possible. He found nothing. Not a hat. Not a glove. Not a boot. Nothing that suggested Jolene had ever been there. He vowed not to quit searching the mountain until Jolene was found. He'd spend every free moment he had looking for her. *At least I'm persistent. At best, an incurable optimist. At worst, a damn old fool. Reminds me. I wanna get me a tattoo.*

He spent his time off at Sugarlands Lodge, where he learned that social media became a *thing*, and *Facebook* was the rage. Storme, his cousin, introduced him to it. With her help, Caleb created his own page, then one all about Jolene. He described her, posted pictures he had taken, shared what he knew, and asked for tips.

He even turned to the Internet for his own searching, volunteered for podcasts, and invited psychics to help. *By gum, who'd a-thought I'd be a techie? An ole mountain man like me, raised in these here hills with the world at my fingertips. Heck, Storme even got me usin' a fancy-dancy phone with a crazy fruit name, includin' all the bells and whistles. I'm connected.*

Caleb caught on quick and learned everything he could about the computer, the Internet, and his phone. If anyone reported a sighting or a clue, he'd followed it up. He even hired a private detective who had retired from the Gatlinburg police department to help with his search.

Before he headed back to LeConte, he paid a visit to a tattoo parlor and got inked. It was a small design to remind him of his quest. He had a photo on his phone that told the artist precisely what he wanted. It only hurt a tad bit.

When Caleb returned to LeConte Lodge, he discovered that the owners had added a few solar power panels. While still primitive and rustic, the lodge had moved a bit more into the 21st century with the added pinch of new-age technology. Caleb made good use of those tools over the years but to no avail.

2012

Auntie Em had mentioned listening to someone named Mariah Windsong, said to be a new-age granny woman, psychic something or other. Caleb wasn't averse to reaching out to her.

Mariah hosted a podcast called *Physic Seekers*, which centered on finding lost connections and forging new ones. Her podcasts discussed many forms of mysticism, including meditation, tarot, and Kabbalah. The podcasts were popular, and Caleb was wise enough to pursue every angle if it led to finding Jolene.

Caleb reached out to Mariah, and she contacted him for an interview via *Skype* after seeing his *Facebook* pleas. He became a frequent visitor to her regularly scheduled podcasts. He cajoled Mariah to keep reporting about Jolene, keeping her alive in the media.

2014

During one interview with Mariah, she asked, "Why do

you keep up the search? By now, you must have lost hope."

Caleb shifted his weight. "Cain't do that. Y'all got to know that Jolene's got guts. She can out hike the llamas she led through these hills. She was no stranger to danger. She knows what to wear, what to do to survive. I think she's out there somewhere. I aim to find her. That feisty female is simply too stubborn to die."

Mariah nodded. "So, you'll continue the search after all these years?"

Caleb looked straight into the camera and nodded. "I'll search for her until the day I die, iffen that's what it takes." He looked down at his tattoo and gave a slight nod, reassuring himself that he'd made the right choice.

"What would you say to her if you find her?"

He corrected with a wink, "*When* I find her, I'll ask, where the hell you been?"

Mariah deadpanned. "You heard it yourself. That's a story of undying love if I've ever heard it. If you have any tips, please notify the Gatlinburg police or tweet to hashtag MariahPsychicSeekers. Be sure to subscribe for the next *Psychic Seekers* podcast."

When the camera turned off, Caleb walked away and said no more. *Not so shore I'd call it* love *anymore. This was never no true love story, but iffen it gets that stubborn woman found, I have no mind to stop it. I feel terrible about letting her go. I shoulda stopped her from goin' off in a huff. Maybe I shoulda just ended things there and then, and I wouldn't have to fret so.*

Mariah headed home after her interview with Caleb. She felt a pressure building inside her, which usually predicted a vision. It always made her head pound. Too bad she didn't have a handy dandy sweat Lodge to retreat into, but she still forced herself to clear her mind.

Once back inside her home, she removed a small vial of

peppermint oil from her bureau drawer. She tipped the vial and anointed her chakras. She lit sage to clear the air and burned tobacco in a small copper bowl to invite her spirit guide to usher her into a deep meditative state. She lit rose incense sticks as well. Taking deep breaths, she began counting backward from a hundred and began to drift away. Despite the heat in the house, the temperature took a sudden drop. Time and space seemed to swirl and then part.

A smoky mist filled the air, and a deep biting cold racked her body. Fine icy rain soaked the frame of someone taking form. The door of her higher consciousness opened and allowed the images pressing her inner eye to take shape.

Mariah shivered and clenched her chattering teeth as a deeper cold enveloped her. White, blazing light assaulted her, momentarily blinding her, yet she felt transported. The icy cold stole her breath when a freezing wind whirled around her.

A plaintive melody she'd heard in past visions underscored the experience, creating infinite sadness to flood her. The energy she felt was feminine when two images took form. One strong and able, the other losing strength.

Once again, the icy rain swirled into a blinding mist. Then it cleared to reveal a young woman huddled upon herself beneath the folds of snow. While in the frozen cocoon, the woman's spirit sank into the abyss. The color bled from her auburn hair, leaving the snow-white strands in its place.

A willowy wraith beckoned the ice-cold woman. She didn't stir much, but a weak pulse continued to beat. A force lifted her. The weakened female spirit hovered between worlds but moved incrementally forward until it merged with the dominant force.

The woman slowly awoke as a blanket of warmth surrounded her. She writhed as if needle pricks forced her to consciousness. Eye still closed, she muttered. "Ca . . ."

Certainty filled Mariah, and she knew she had found Jolene. She wasn't dead. Unfortunately, that was all Mariah could process before she too succumbed to the healing, soothing warmth and slipped into a deep sleep.

Mariah awoke famished and nursed the resultant remnant of a throbbing headache from her vision. When it lifted, she congratulated herself. She was right. There was more she could do to help Caleb. She sent him a text.

*Jolene is alive. She survived the storm. White is what I saw. Does that mean anything to you?*

Caleb's response was immediate.

*White? What the hell? Nope. Brings nuthin' to mind.*

# Chapter Fifteen: When Will I See You Again?

2015

Caleb intensified his search. He had to find Jolene. The guilt was eating him alive. *Why did I push her? Why couldn't I leave well enough alone? I knew she wasn't into commitments. It's all my fault. I drove her away. Dagnabbit. If only . . . if only . . . if only. I'm getting nowhere with this line of thought.* He sighed and pushed forward.

After Mariah's text, Caleb felt Jolene had to be in the vicinity. *Maybe all that white indicated snow.* He spent more time retracing the paths she might have taken. The NPS now required backcountry hikers to register their routes. He was savvy enough to be sure his whereabouts were known to Park officials every time he went out. *Too bad we didn't have to register our llama train. Don't want them losing me like we lost Jolene.*

Once on the trail, Caleb pondered how Jolene might have survived and where she could possibly be. The panniers held MRS packs, and she habitually carried a full canteen. She might have taken a wrong turn. Could she have stumbled onto another trail? If so, she could be anywhere. Or had she become disoriented and got lost in the wilderness? Even so, she could have found some hunting cabin or a trapper outside the National Park and contacted someone. Part of him never allowed even the merest thought of all that energy extinguished. He refused to consider it. Besides, Mariah said she was still alive.

For some reason, he was drawn — even compelled — to re-hike the Boulevard Trail. He didn't know why, but his gut told him he was onto something — some link, some clue about Jolene's disappearance.

When Caleb reached the junction linking the Boulevard Trail to the Appalachian Trail, Ranger Luke Scraper caught up to him.

Sorrow filled Luke's eyes. He led Caleb to a rocky outcrop, laid his hand on Caleb's shoulder, forcing him to sit. "Caleb, I'm sorry to be the one to bring y'all this news. Miss Emma Jean passed away."

Disbelief coupled with grief swept through Caleb's whole body. He shook his head, then raised a hand to his face and let the pain — strong enough to make him insane — loose and free. He didn't give a whit about what anyone thought about his breakdown.

Luke pulled Caleb's head into his chest, patting him in consolation and shared grief. Luke and the whole town knew, loved, and would mourn Emma Jean.

Caleb found his face dripping with tears on the ride to the family Lodge. He swiped his flannel shirt across his wet face and did the best he could to cope with his loss. Seemed like he was destined to lose those he loved. First his ma, then Millie, Uncle Jake, Jolene, even his beloved Tater, too. And now his Auntie Em.

When they arrived at the Lodge, Caleb's cousins, Skye, Storme, and Sunny, were sitting at a table on the veranda and appeared to be conferring with the family attorney. From their expressions, they were devastated and having a hard time.

Millie found him climbing the steps to the front entrance and drew him into her arms. She filled him in, giving the bare facts and trying to answer his questions, all while holding him close and tight. His heart hurt, but Millie's touch always helped to calm him.

Funeral plans were made. Neighbors came and went. Caleb buried himself in his cabin beneath the quilt that Emma Jean had made for him and grieved. When he briefly emerged, Skye grabbed his hand and pulled him to a private spot.

Skye pressed a locket into his hands. "It has your mom's hair inside, along with pictures of Gram and your mom. She'd want you to have it now."

Caleb mumbled his thanks, flipped it open, saw the copper hair, and wept again.

Caleb didn't trust himself not to break down during the funeral, so he didn't venture into the church when the services began. Nor did he join the family at the gravesite for the burial, where even the mountain sky cried along with him. Instead, he retreated into the Smoky Mountain trees, where the dripping leaves shielded him from view. His harmonica revealed his grief, letting everyone know he was nearby.

In time, he retreated to his pickup truck, where he dried off and removed his fiddle from its case to play one last time for his beloved Auntie Em. Each note bled for his loss.

He just couldn't face this loss, couldn't deal with the sympathy. With Auntie Em's sudden death, the boy inside Caleb took the last step into real manhood. Any trace of the boy he once was, was gone as surely as the tears coursing down his cheeks. Emma Jean had been the one constant in his life, the mother he hadn't had.

Had Tater been alive, she'd have shared his sorrow. But she, too, had passed just like all the others he loved. Tater would have licked his face, trying to console him. He wished she and Emma Jean were there, but all he had left was a locket with a strand of hair and a picture and Tater's collar.

His cousin John was in the throes of grief, too, as was the whole family, the entire town. Emma Jean Weathers had been a mainstay for the community, one of the wisest of the granny women. The anchor for many was gone, and the life Caleb knew was gone as well.

2016

Caleb retreated to his hilltop hideaway at LeConte Lodge. He no longer accompanied any llama trains and hadn't for years. He was too busy entertaining guests and conducting day hikes, but his time off was still spent searching for the flaming auburn-haired beauty. Jolene was mountain strong and mountain tough, but so was he. Looking for her gave him permission and purpose, a reason to carry on and live.

The lodge had just closed for the season, and Caleb had started his winter caretaking again when a fire broke out on Chimney Tops Mountain. He could see the smoke from the LeConte Lodge, which overlooked the entire event. He knew he'd never forget the sight of actual smoke spreading across the mountain tops. It wasn't Smoky Mountain mist this time. It was real smoke.

After a couple days, the fires spread and grew closer to Le-Conte. Park fire officials ordered him to evacuate. When he made it down the mountain, he was shocked to see the devastation. He learned that strong southerly winds were still spreading burning embers, knocking down trees, which hit power lines, creating more fires.

The fire had jumped across Cherokee Orchard Road. Thankfully, it hadn't even scorched the Bud Ogle primitive pioneer cabin, but down the road a piece, the entire hillside had succumbed to the flames. Caleb bowed his head and mourned the mountain. He wept for it and its children, the trees, birds, rabbits, deer, and bears. So much beauty consumed and gone.

The granny women claimed for every loss, there was a gain. Caleb had found one amongst the devastation. In many ways, the fire-damaged hills would be easier to search, because the underbrush was gone.

When he was allowed back up to LeConte Lodge, he continued his searching. On one trip to town for supplies, he swore he had found Jolene. *At last!* Her long auburn locks were pulled in a ponytail through the back of her baseball cap. He raced to her and turned her to face him. Only to find that the gal was definitely not Jolene. Nor was she amused.

Thinking about his mistake later, he had to remind himself that Jolene was no longer the *young* woman who had disappeared. By now, she would have also aged much as he had. The gray in his beard and scattered throughout his brown hair definitely showed his age.

Unfortunately, mistaken identity happened too many times to count when he ventured down to Gatlinburg and Pigeon Forge. As a result of the podcasts and Facebook posts and news updates, people had begun to report sightings of her everywhere, from Wears Cove to the Cataloochee section of the Park out near Asheville, North Carolina. *Heck, one of the lodge crew claimed he spotted her in Florida!* Every reported encounter led to dead ends, false hopes that killed him bit by bit.

Every time a body was found anywhere, Caleb prayed it wasn't Jolene. He had heard stories of a red-haired woman living with a Cherokee male. *Jolene? Living with a man? Unlikely, but who knew? Stranger things had happened. If Jolene hooked up with any male, it'd have been me.* He had doubted the report but followed all leads. He'd found the redhead, but the woman was *not* Jolene. He constantly consoled himself by recalling Mariah's texting that Jolene was alive.

Other stories circulated that Jolene was married with children. Some heard for sure she was the social worker out at Cooke County. Maybe she was that gal they arrested over in Maryville? Speculations ran rampant. Resulting in nothing. Every now and again, a reporter would interview Caleb on TV to keep the story alive, but nothing ever panned out.

2020

Caleb continued working at LeConte Lodge during the COVID-19 breakout. There was no need to come down Mount LeConte and risk exposure. The helicopter had made its usual early March drop. So when the Park had locked down at the end of March, he had more than enough supplies to last him through quarantine in this mountain haven.

Caleb's cellphone wasn't much use on top of LeConte. Signals often failed there and in the surrounding mountains, but he could periodically get news on his phone. Once in a blue moon, he managed to get a call through, which was how he knew his cousins were quarantined at Sugarlands Lodge and safe.

He never regretted the solar power linking LeConte Lodge to limited contact with the outside world. What he managed to hear about the toll COVID-19 took was disheartening and sad. Even isolated on Mount LeConte, he couldn't ignore the rising death toll worldwide. More than once, he was glad there was no television up there.

He couldn't search for Jolene in town during the lockdown, but he had begun to suspect she was off the grid. Maybe somewhere living a good life. Still, it bothered him not knowing. The unknown was agony. Worse than knowing for sure, he suspected. He had no form of closure, and that drove him crazy. *Was she hospitalized with the coronavirus somewhere?* There was no way to know. As far as he knew, there was no list of individual COVID deaths nationwide. *Was she a Jane Doe somewhere?*

Caleb had loved and lost—twice. He was aging and grew too cynical to chase a phantom love who never returned his ardor in the first place. He just wished he knew where she was. Her disappearance haunted him.

Caleb couldn't help where his mind wandered next. Thinking of Jolene's disappearance had lowered his guard. Now, thoughts about Tater and losing her surfaced. That little rascal wouldn't let him sit without cuddling in his lap. The girl would poke his newspaper until the only way to get peace was to bring her up on his lap and read to her. Somehow, the memory of her broke through his last defense, allowing him to cry.

When he'd buried Tater, he'd placed one of his socks near her mouth, so his fur baby had a piece of him with her always. *Can't believe how much I loved that dog. She's the only fountain of joy and unconditional love I ever had. All I had to do was just exist. She brought my heart back to life and showed me I could love again. And I did only to lose – again. One heartache after another.*

There had been something special between him and his dog . . . He'd cried harder and longer for her than he had over people. Had Tater been there, she'd have sighed, nuzzled her snout into him, and lapped his tears away before distracting him by snatching something she shouldn't have. He missed her like crazy. He seldom permitted himself to think of her, but this time, it served to set something loose inside him.

Tater had lived twenty years—unusual for her breed—but the joy and comfort she had given him was beyond belief. He had buried her at Myrtle Point, in the grove where he had found some peace and love with Jolene. Tater had led him there one day as she chased a boomer, a mini squirrel inhabiting the top of LeConte.

He went to her grave and wept bitterly for everyone. There was no one to hear him sob except his God, mountain, and

Tater. He pulled out his harmonica and played until the sunset bled into the purple night. The Dog Star seemed particularly bright as he gazed at the night sky. Despite his grief, he laughed at the irony. Tater had found a way to comfort him using starlight and a constellation.

The wind whispered to him in its insidious tree talk way, *Gooo. Mooove. Ooon.* Maybe he would. He'd get through this pandemic and leave LeConte at the end of the season.

Caleb swore he heard Tater's snort of approval mixed with the tree talk as he made his way back to his bunk.

# Chapter Sixteen: Here You Come Again

Caleb knew the time had come at last. Long ago, he had stopped making the strenuous trek up and down the mountains to focus on running the LeConte Lodge. He was facing his seventies, and it was long past time to head down for good.

For years he'd given himself permission to make futile and unproductive searches within and outside the GSMNP and still had not found Jolene. It was time to give it up. Some good did come out of it—like the Bible and granny women said. He'd found a satisfying career and detailed knowledge of the park's 800 miles of trails.

His thoughts wandered as he hiked down the mountain. *I never planned to be a confirmed bachelor, but here I am, killing it.* Caleb shook his head and wondered about just how exactly that had happened. *Somehow the years flew by, and I just never met a wife, a soulmate, or even someone that rocked my world down to my socks.* Even as he thought it, he knew that wasn't true.

Someone had got to his heart fifty-some years ago. And someone else more recently than that. Both had caused him pain. Millie and then Jolene. So much heartache. Even getting away from everything atop Mount LeConte didn't stop Cupid from aiming for him, striking him in the heart.

Caleb shrugged his shoulders and adjusted the weight of the backpack he wore to make this trip down the mountain. He wasn't taking the usual trail, though. No, this time, he took the long and winding Boulevard Trail, a branch off the famous Appalachian Trail that led to LeConte Lodge. It was scenic and lent itself to contemplation. He needed the time this hike took so he could think straight. He needed to figure out where he planned to spend his winter years and what he wanted to do with the rest of his life.

While most folks had retired years earlier, Caleb was not into that. Not now. Not anytime soon. Not while he was still fit and trim. The muscles in his arms, legs, and back had years left in them. Retirement sounded weak to him, like he was finished. Besides, he was in no way ready to rock in any chair anytime soon. He wondered if he ever would be. He rubbed at the stubble of several days surrounding his chin. Reviewing his life, he recalled the years spent at another lodge, the Sugarlands Lodge. Another piece of paradise.

Caleb knew he would again be exchanging one lodge for another, coming full circle. Still in paradise but back home at the Sugarlands Lodge from whence he came. He'd happily spent decades on LeConte, but several factors forced his hand again. Auntie Em's death, his advancing age, and the overwhelming need for closure drove him back.

His young cousins had taken over managing the Lodge upon Emma Jean's sudden death. He had kept in touch with them over the years. Somewhere near the end of 2019, Skye had mentioned that Herman Trentham, Millie's man, had died from what they thought was the flu that turned into pneumonia. Part of him had perked up when he learned Millie still worked for the Lodge.

Caleb finished the final leg of the trail, found his pickup truck where he'd left it, and drove down Newfound Gap Road, but not for the last time. He still had things to settle up at LeConte, but he also had something he needed to do at the Lodge first. Before he could begin a new chapter in his life, he had to finish two from his past. One was Jolene. The other,

Millie.

Caleb drove to the Sugarlands Lodge, which the locals knew simply as the Lodge. Instead of being greeted by Auntie Em, as in the days preceding her death, he spied Emmie Jo Trentham Maples, his old flame's now married daughter. He'd known her from birth, and here *she* was married with grown kids of her own. *Hell, I've heard tell that Millie's about to become a great-grandmother. No chance of that for me – ever. What would it have been like to young'uns of my own?* He shook those thoughts off. *No sense thinkin' on it. Tweren't meant to be. That's all there is to that.*

Caleb walked through the front entrance of the Lodge, noting the amenities were far better than the old days. The refurbished fountain splashed clear stream water, the geraniums contrasted nicely with the green shutters, and the old rockers and porch swings lent charm of the old to bleed through the renovations.

Emmie Jo, a redhead with a great smile and sparkling green eyes, greeted him. "Hey, Mister 'Leb, how y'all doin'?"

Caleb tipped his old, battered hat. "Right well. Thought I'd come down here a spell. Where's Sunny?"

Emmie Jo nodded. "She's flittin' around here somewhere. She's so hard to pin down seein's how she a mom now. I think she's in the family quarters nursin' her young'un" She must have seen his reaction. "TMI, eh? You don't need that information, I guess. Stayin' in the usual? Caretaker's Cottage?"

With a deep sigh of contentment, Caleb smiled a *yes* and sat in a new armchair in the Lodge Great Room, taking in the magnificent hand-carved staircase. "Ah thought ah might. Where's your twin?"

"She's at her new job."

Caleb hadn't heard about it. "That so? Where at?"

"Bar None."

His brow rose. "Yer kiddin' me. That ole place still goin'?"

"Goin' strong. Y'all oughta stop in. Take yer fiddle. It's

open mic night. I hear tell that ole Wailin' Wally O'Toole is over there. Oughta give 'em some hell with that old fiddle."

"Thank ye kindly. I'll think on it. Yer ma in the kitchen?"

"Where else would she be? G'wan in and see her. I think she'll take kindly to that."

Hmm. "Maybe I will." *Geesh, now I'm soundin' like Jolene.* The thought ate at him, so he put on his big boy pants and wandered in.

He wanted to appear all casual like, nice and easy-peasy. He crossed his feet at the ankle and lounged against the kitchen doorframe, gazing at Millie's still fit form. He removed his hat and twisted it by the brim, having second thoughts about entering Millie's domain. He had heard she was territorial about it. "Howdy, Millie. What's cookin'?"

Millie jumped and raised a hand to her chest. "Damn, man. You gave me a start! I have a mind to scramble you just like this mess of eggs for almost givin' me a heart attack. What do ye think yer doin'?"

Caleb straightened up fast, nervously twisting his hat in his hands. "I wasn't fixin' on scarin' ye none. What kind of greeting would that be?"

"A mighty unwelcome one, I'd say. Whaddya want?"

"Just some coffee and chit-chat. Ye gonna deny me that after all these years?"

"Thought Emmie Jo was seein' to ye. Gonna hafta have a word with her. What's she thinkin'?"

He drawled out his words. "Weeell, I reckon she'd say, *Git yer sorry self in there and say hey.*" Caleb knew he'd got to her since she had lapsed into the strong dialect of her girlhood.

Millie snorted. "I'd say you've done that."

"I'm jist doin' a kindness. I'm sorry about Herman makin' y'all a widow woman."

"Been a widow since COVID-19 struck. I'm thinkin' it wasn't pneumonia but the coronavirus that took Herman."

She raised a shaky finger to flick the sudden moisture from her eyes.

Caleb looked her straight in the eye. "Don't matter what they call it. His loss is the cost. I'm mighty sorry to hear that. I just wanted to say *sorry* is all."

Millie harrumphed and poured him a cup of coffee. "I thank you for that. It's true. It's hard. He wasn't no young buck like his boys these days, but he was still goin' strong when he got took down. It was godawful fast. Why it didn't get me is a wonder. The kids are all out the house and grown, and they're fine. We all got the new vaccine shots so . . ." She visibly shook herself and looked at him. Then she yelled for Emmie Jo to take over.

As they left the room, Caleb noticed Sunny with her baby strapped into some doohickey over her chest, nodded to her, and followed Millie out to the veranda. She walked to the far end and gestured to a rocking chair. They sat.

She cleared her throat. "About time we clear the air. I owe you that much."

He nodded and then spoke. "No need. Life happened."

She nodded. "We happened, too."

Caleb stopped rocking. "No need to discuss the past, girlie."

Millie looked at him. A new light appeared in her eyes. "Some words just need sayin'."

"Not after all these years. We can just be civil since I'm comin' down the mountain. Goin' to start a new life down here."

Millie nodded. "All the more reason to say what I've got to say."

"Doesn't all have to be said in one sittin'."

Millie looked at him with regret in her eyes. "After I have my say, there might not be any more sittin'."

"Look, I'm not into re-livin' the past. What do ye say, we

just enjoy this beautiful mountain morning? Why ruin a beautiful day? I don't need any more than that."

She nodded. "We'll table it, then. "

"Or simply agree to disagree. Let tomorrow take care of itself. On the other hand, you been out to Bar None?"

She laughed. "Who hasn't?"

"Me. That's who. How 'bout we go tonight? For old-time's sake."

"Just like that? After all these years?"

He snapped his fingers. "Yes'm. Jist like that. Wanna catch a burger first at the Huddle House?"

Her bright laughter burst from her throat. She nodded. "What a blast from the past. You're on."

He looked at her and winked. "It's a date."

She swatted at him but missed.

"See ye at sundown, then."

A look crossed her face, but he didn't know what to make of it. As he walked away, he tossed his remarks over his shoulder. "No big deal. I'm not lookin' for a happy endin'. Life's no fairytale, I know."

Millie smiled. "Sure. That's what they all say."

*Was Millie flirting with me? Am I flirting back?*

He nodded and tipped his hat, then made his way to his cabin. He'd be staying there until he figured out what he wanted to do. He had brought his fiddle down the last time he was here. It waited for him in its case. He rosined his bow, tuned up the strings, and began to play a lively, happy tune. He felt great. *Son of a gun, I been so used to playin' for folks up LeConte and lookin' for Jolene, I just about plumb forgot about that ole bar.* He began to play *Old Mother Leary* and decided he'd be having a hot time in the old town bar that night.

# CHAPTER SEVENTEEN: I SAW HER FACE

Caleb opened the door of his pickup for Millie. Surprisingly, Millie was dressed in jeans and wore a red-checkered lumberjack shirt cinched at the waist. Her full breasts displayed the tiniest bit of cleavage. She smelled like vanilla and cinnamon.

She smiled. "I see you still drive a red pickup."

He laughed. "This here's an F-150."

"Boys and their toys. I know all about that."

Caleb rocked on his feet. "What red-blooded American southern boy wouldn't update to this beauty?"

Millie threw her hands out and shrugged.

Caleb was surprised to see the city sprawl. While once Bar None had been *out a piece* from Wears Valley, the cityscape had spread, and new shops lined the road. Bar None still boasted its signature red neon sign, and the windows still leached warm light out. He spied some classic cars and several motorcycles parked nearby.

When he got out of his truck, foot-stompin' toe-tapping fiddle music told him Wally was present. He straightened his shoulders and led Millie inside. People were dancin', hootin', and hollerin' just like the old days. He spied a woman with short white hair dancin' up a storm, reminding him of the old days when Jolene was there. Strictly out of habit, his eyes scanned the joint. Nope. No flaming auburn hair, no ivory skin, no emerald-green eyes in sight. He sauntered up to the old bar.

A familiar redhead greeted him. "What's your pleasure?"

He gave her a shame-shame gesture. "What's a nice girl like y'all doin' in a place like this, Miss Joy June? Don't y'all know better than to ask that question? Could get you into some hot water."

"Mister 'Leb! Don't you worry none. I'm fine." Joy June pulled out a baseball bat. "This will knock some sense into any knucklehead who gets out of line." She jerked her head and thumb back where a burly man stepped up and laughed. "And Bufford here will knock 'em into next week when I'm done." She smiled at her mother.

He took a seat at the bar and turned to listen to his old rival play.

Millie ordered for the two of them. "One drink with two olives on a stick, please, and one Appletini."

Caleb heard her and let a loud laugh fly. "Shaken not stirred. That's my line, right, barkeep?"

Joy June winked. " Yep. All except my title. Nowadays, it's called mixologist." She turned her attention to her mother. "Y'all mean a Martini for Caleb, Ma?"

Millie grinned. "Yep, that Yankee drink. But for me, I'll have the Appletini."

Caleb nodded and replied, "Ah stands corrected. Sorry, Missy Mixologist."

Wally played a set of some old favorites with a nod to his signature pieces.

"Ain't lost his touch none," Caleb said in an aside to Joy June.

After the set was done and the jukebox played, Wally joined him. He stretched out a hand to shake it.

"Mister O'Toole," Joy June warned. "How many times I got to tell ya. Fist bumps. Social distancing."

Caleb sprang up. "To hell with that. Ain't no way to greet an old friend like him." He gave the man an ole country boy bear hug.

"Damn! If it ain't the fiddlin' mountain man hisself," Wally said amid the hug. "How's it hangin'?"

Caleb laughed. "Hangin' just fine, thank ye. That was some mighty fine playin'."

Wally tipped his ever-present black cowboy hat in thanks. "Ye feelin' up to playin'?"

Caleb nodded his head. "Don't mind if I do."

"You aim to fiddlin' that gal next to you into love?"

Caleb took a sip, wiped his mouth, and said, "I'll fiddle the buttons off yer shirt first. See how that goes, and we'll see."

Wally guffawed. "Is that a true fact? See that gal over there?"

He nodded

"I'm going to play *her* into love. That fella she's with is sweet on her. Her? Not so much."

"If anyone can, you can." Caleb threw a questioning glance at Millie. "Wanna dance?"

He and Millie danced a slow one, and damned if she didn't feel good in his arms. She was a perfect fit. He heard her breath catch, and time stood still. Could Wally's boast be true? Was he planning on fiddlin' Millie and him back into love, too?

Caleb felt something change deep within his soul. Something melted and dissolved away. All of a sudden, he felt a weight lift from his belly, his shoulders, his life. He felt free of the burden he'd carried around all these years.

He drank his fill and sat back to enjoy the music. Damned if Wally didn't play the most romantic song that him wondering. *Maybe I could fall in love again.* He bent his head and kissed Millie for the first time in fifty years. He didn't think twice about it. He just did it. He stole a kiss from his old sweetheart and knew it was good. He shocked himself silly. *Tarnation! Didn't know I was gonna up and do that!*

Millie's fingers flew to her mouth. She grinned. "It's about time."

Caleb winked at her. During the set change, the white-haired woman slipped out. He turned to Bufford. "Sumthin' familiar about that gal, but danged iffen I know where I seen her afore."

Bufford, with a nod in her direction, said, "In your dreams, man. That's Jo, and she don't stick with anyone long enough for us folks to know much more about her. Holds her liquor, I'll tell ye that much."

Then it was his turn to play, and Caleb had other things to do than thinkin' on some strange woman. Fueled by Millie's returned kiss, he picked up his bow and fiddle after mounting the harmonica in its holder. He launched into *Mustang Sally* and followed that with *Elvira*. Caleb had everyone on their feet.

Wally yelled out, "Boy, y'all just played the worms straight outta the ground, you did!"

Caleb laughed and tipped his bow in response, and fist-bumped him. Joy June couldn't reprimand him this time.

Caleb bowed and took a draw of the cold draft someone gave him—he was parched, and no sissy drink could do him what a cold brew could. He glanced Millie's way and damned if he didn't plan to make-out like teenagers when he got her home.

Once he turned the truck off and put the gear into park, Millie took the lead by gently kissing his lips and savoring them as if losing herself in the act. She ran her fingers through his hair, combing it with a light touch. Then using her pointer finger, she traced his jawline.

Caleb opened his mouth, tasting her while his tongue explored and enjoyed her flavor, her mix of cinnamon and sugar. He licked her bottom lip and drew it into his mouth. On second taste, maybe she reminded him of sourwood honey. His lips traveled across her face. He cupped it with his hands, kissed her sweet lips, and then gently each eye.

Millie responded and drew further into his body, pulling him closer into her.

Caleb made sure the kiss was hot enough for her to feel the heat and his evident ardor.

Millie ran her hands up under his shirt and fiddled with his chest hairs, making him moan. Then — as if she suddenly remembered where they were — she straightened. "Why are we behaving like love-struck kids? This is not the place."

"Yer right as usual, ole gal."

She play-punched him. "I'll have you know I'm not old. I am a queen-ager, and I'm drawin' the line. That's all."

Caleb felt crestfallen. "Queen-ager, eh? What in tarnation is that?"

"That be a senior teenager. With a crown." Millie's eyes gleamed. "That's it. All ye git . . . for now."

The following morning Caleb met Millie over breakfast. He felt kindlier toward her. More at ease, relaxed, and — dared he say — happy? They fell back into an old rhythm. Running into each other here and there. Around the Lodge. In the Park. In town. Even at the Food City. He didn't hide, nor did he abandon his cart when they ended up in the frozen food section. They both reached for the Rocky Road at the same time, their hands touching. Zap! *Was that tingling due to the frozen food or from touching Millie's hand?* They each drew their hands back fast.

Millie giggled and fanned her face as if suddenly very hot. "Hubba, hubba."

He made a slight bow and waved her forward. "After y'all, ma'am, ladies first."

Millie took the pint. "Thank you, kind sir."

Caleb looked at the measly pint longingly. "Y'all gonna eat that all by yerself?"

She smiled. "Apparently not. Y'all are lickin' your chops like a hound dog tryin' to nab himself a bone. Why don't we have it for dessert?"

A long slow smile worked its way across Caleb's face. *Rather have y'all.*

After Millie paid for the ice cream, she looked at him. "Meet me at Mynatt Park? This will never make it home. Too hot outside."

He nodded and got inside his truck, watching Millie climb into her SUV.

The city was renovating the park, so they had to walk a fair piece before they found an undisturbed table beside the foot-bridge and sat down. Using the plastic spoons Caleb found in his truck, they shared the ice cream straight from the carton as daylight faded and the light of the fireflies began to flash. Caleb couldn't believe how right he felt. How settled. How at home. How pleased. Noticing a trace of ice cream dotting the side of Millie's mouth, he wiped it away, then sucked the cream off his finger and sought her sweet lips for a kiss. He pulled back, but Millie edged closer to him and initiated the next longer, sweeter, hot kiss.

He had intended to give and get a simple sweet kiss, but this one was surprisingly both calming and exciting. Refreshingly cool yet passionately hot. Sweet but with a hint of spice, danger, and thrills. Satisfying but demanding more.

"That was a long time comin'." Millie looked pleased as a cat curled up on a mat.

Hand in hand, they strolled the park and ended up facing the stream. Millie paused, approached a gray back, and shared the seat it provided with Caleb. She toed off her shoes to let the cool water tickle her toes as it gurgled its way through the rock-strewn pass.

Caleb did the same. Every now and again, he bent to pick up a stone and skipped it across a small pool formed between two huge boulders. He plucked a strand of sweet grass to chaw on, but he tossed it away with impatience. He shoved his hands in his pockets, at a loss for something to say.

They remained silent, listening to the flow of the stream providing its own symphony. The silence was broken only by the sound of the water and the enchanting cicada trills that accompanied it. A breeze stirred the trees. *What do they have to say about us?* He hoped it sighed *yeeesss.* The music of nature made him happy and at peace.

Then Millie turned to him. "Too bad we didn't bring a picnic supper. Y'all hungry?"

"Yep."

Millie got playful and batted her eyes. "How' bout I fry up some chicken for dinner at my place?"

Caleb flashed a huge smile. "I reckon that'd be mighty fine."

"Y'all hafta help, hear?"

"Loud and clear. Woman, I been cookin' for years on top of Ole Smoky, I reckon I can peel a tater or two."

"You're on! It's a deal."

Caleb and Millie got in their respective vehicles and drove to Millie's place. It had the look of a comfy but tidy rambling farmhouse. The screen door slammed when they entered. Caleb looked at the broken spring and made a note to fix it when he got a chance. He hadn't run maintenance at both lodges for nothing.

That was when he realized he'd do anything for her. His feelings, dormant for so long, forged through his defenses, and the love he'd locked down came flowing out. He felt his rapidly healing heart pounding in his chest.

Millie donned an apron, so Caleb looked around for another. The only one available hung on a hook. It was a fancy one with ruffles. Millie laughed out loud when she saw him donning the frilly thing.

Caleb grinned. "Real men wear ruffles. I don't see no *Kiss the Cook* manly-man barbeque aprons, so this will have to do." He paraded around her kitchen, modeling it.

Millie directed him to the potato bin and tossed a peeler at him.

He caught it. "You've got a good arm. Ever play baseball?"

She laughed. "With three sons, that'd be a yes."

"Three boys? How'd I miss that?"

"Must have been holed up on top of ole Smoky. Had me Abraham, and then a year later, Lincoln."

"You named two boys after the president?"

She arched her brow and puffed out her chest like a riled hognose snake. "I like the names. And the man. Plus, it was fun to play with the names. You got a problem with that?"

He chuckled."Jist see the humor in it."

Millie giggled. "Can't blame me for gettin' my jollies where I can find 'em."

Caleb granted her that and turned on his playlist while Millie retrieved the utensils and ingredients they'd need. *The Tennessee Waltz* played, and he grabbed her, dancing and twirling her in circles. He did not hold her in the traditional waltz style but drew her into his body as close as he could.

Millie giggled. "Y'all pack a handgun, Mister Weathers, or are y'all just happy to see me?"

In response, Caleb twirled and dipped her, then raised her and gave her a kiss designed to curl her toes. He deepened the kiss, took her hand, and placed it on his hardening, throbbing cock. She stroked him, then loosened his belt and began to unzip him . . .

Caleb's cock sprang forth in greeting. This time there were no surprised giggles like there had been the first time she'd seen his dick spring into action. This time her experienced fingers knew precisely what to do. Their clothes went flying as they peeled them off, forgetting all about potatoes and chicken.

Millie found his balls and played with them. He backed her onto the kitchen table, then sat her down on it, sweeping whatever was there away. He ran his fingers through her locks like he had when they were teens, inhaling her strawberry-scented strands.

Millie panted and held a hand up. "Caleb, I fear I'm a retread virgin."

Caleb slowed. "What?"

"It's been a long, long time since . . ."

"Hush. Same here. Be gentle with me, woman."

She giggled.

He made a slow, kissing descent as he caressed each and every spot on her well-kept, pleasantly rounded body. Age might have taken its toll, but her skin was supple and soft. Her hips flared more than he remembered, but that didn't faze him. No more than his silver chest hair detracted from his still hale and ready erection. Which was a relief. He was far from the young buck he once was, but he had a strong desire to fuck this woman in his arms. From what he saw, he had nothing at all to wish were any different.

He stroked the inside of her legs, kissing her thighs while taking his time. He added the wetness of his mouth to her center to release the hot flood of her youth. He kept his kisses and caresses consistent until her honey dripped for his pleasure.

"Wow! Caleb! Oh, my God, you're driving me crazy. I don't think I've ever been so wet."

"Good." Caleb used his hands to bring Millie to a climax. He let her savor it as her body shuddered, but it wasn't long before he had to enter her.

Face to face, Caleb finally took Millie like he wished he had fifty years ago. While a current of ecstasy raced through his system, he deliberately slowed down, taking his time, trying hard to hold off his climax. He wanted to savor each sensation, taste supple lips, the thrill of having a dream fulfilled. He had waited such a long, long time for Millie. A lifetime, really. He wanted to prolong this wondrous moment for as long as possible. It was no easy feat, especially since they had never gone straight to home base together before. He aimed to make their *first time* memorable.

Before either could climax again, Caleb pulled out, parted her trembling legs, and licked her innermost lips, driving her wild. Then he stopped. He had to shift positions when age intruded. She seemed to welcome the shift, too. Then he started with his deep, deep kisses. His lips demanded more.

Mille's red-hot heat poured from her, making him boil with need and desire. Love delayed was very sweet and well worth the wait. He kissed her like he had never kissed anyone before. He sucked, suckled, bit, nipped, and caressed every inch of her lush body.

Her response was appreciative and noisy.

Driven by Millie's groans, moans, and cries, Caleb attempted to do everything he could to send her straight into ecstasy. What he accomplished was more than merely rinse and repeat.

He found himself falling in love with Millie all over again. He had survived all these years not by denying his love for her. Instead, he had accepted that he did love her but had locked it away in the deepest part of his heart, soul, and psyche. He'd stayed away as much as possible in the past so he wouldn't rip the scar open. But now, he sensed true healing working its way into his heart.

As they continued, Millie's lips met his whenever possible. She drank him in as he entered her hot folds. He slowly pulled out, then repeated the process for some glorious heart-stopping moments while he nestled her in his embrace.

In a surprise move, she wrapped her legs around him. He

stood—briefly laughing—as he struggled to drive deep within her, impaling her with his ready-to-burst cock. But it was soon clear he had to lower her to the floor onto the rag rug first. Aging was a reality after all. They giggled as he drove them both into heaven. Breathing hard, he rolled off her and lay on his back panting.

Millie fanned her flushed face. "Lawd have mercy! That was worth the wait."

Caleb swiped at the mess he'd made between Millie's thighs and licked his fingers. "Now that there? That was finger-lickin' good. Ready for round two?"

Millie laughed. "Looks like we should order a pizza and rethink dessert." She winked.

The next time Caleb found Millie, she was perched on the porch swing, ready to watch the setting sun. He joined her, letting his body touch hers as he sat beside her. They talked as the sky exploded with a fiery sunset. He regaled her with his exploits, which seemed to please her.

Later over her famous peach cobbler, he discovered a certain peace and compatibility that he wasn't going to fuss about. They were beyond their past, so he might as well enjoy her company in the present. No sense dwelling on yesterday. What was once lost was now found, and he was content to go with the flow. *Let nature take its course.*

Millie, with pride in her voice, spoke about her children. "My life's been really all about them. I'm not complaining. My lot in life's been good. I miss Herman. He went so fast. I hardly blinked, and that was it . . . It was a mercy, I reckon. How 'bout you? Seems you enjoyed your traispin' and wanderin' and wranglin'? I recall you playin' the Fiddle Fests, too."

Caleb smiled. "Took me out of state several times competing. That was interesting. Saw the big city. Saw the ocean once or twice, but I was always happiest home here in these mountains."

"Good thing. You ever miss havin' a wife and kids?"

He filled with remorse and sighed. "Wasn't meant to be. Never found anything that lasted. Had sumthin' with a gal named Jolene —"

Millie gasped. "The woman who went missin', ye mean? The one on TV?"

Caleb nodded. "The very same. Lost in the big blizzard. Combed these hills lookin' for her. Never did find her. Reckon I've looked long enough. Ye can only carry a torch so far before it burns out. She must be dead or as good as. Can't find her, and I'm done lookin'. So, no mini-Calebs running around these or any other parts of the country."

"Was she like that song Dolly sings?"

He laughed. "Well, now, she did have pale skin, emerald eyes, and auburn hair."

Millie grinned, and a light twinkled in her eyes. She winked. "Did she take ye just because she could?"

Caleb nodded. "I reckon she did. Jist not for life."

"Whaddya mean?"

"Wasn't into marryin'. Was wanting to be footloose and fancy-free. Go where the wind blows. Adventure."

Millie stared at him for a moment, then smiled. "It's my good fortune she wasn't the marryin' kind."

He grinned and suggested they go for a walk.

It was easy to walk beside Millie under the spreading green trees along the stream. Easy to throw a penny in the wishing well and lose track of time together. Easy to be with each other again as if they had never been apart.

Millie spoke in a tone mellow and low. "Hank's livin' in California. Abraham went into the army, and Lincoln's itchin' to join him. And you've seen my girls. Don't rightly think Joy June's ever gonna settle down, and Emmie Jo's walkin' in my shoes. Had herself a mess of kids, 'cept *she* married her high school sweetheart."

They meandered, quiet for a while, then Caleb said, "Ye actually did marry yer high school boyfriend."

She shook her head. "My high school sweetheart was you. I didn't marry *you*." Millie stretched out her hand and touched him. "I've missed you, Caleb. Splittin' up with you was hard to do."

"Seriously? Shore looked durn easy to me. I dunno —"

"There's a lot you don't know."

Caleb looked at her.

Millie's lower lip trembled. "Before we get involved any further, there's sumthin' y'all should know." Her eyes filled.

Caleb stopped her. "Don't need no confession, Millie. What's done is done. What's past is past. All that doesn't stop what's goin' on here now."

Millie looked serious. "We'll see. After I tell you, life will never be the same again."

"Just spit it out, Millie."

"You have family —"

He nodded. "Most folks do have kin. I've got John and Marsha and their lot."

Millie hesitated, then took a deep breath. "You have kids, too. You are a father."

"What's that you say? Whaddya mean?"

"My twins are yours."

# CHAPTER EIGHTEEN: I CAN SEE CLEARLY NOW

Caleb shook Millie by the shoulders. "What? What twins?" Millie bit her lip, trembling beneath his touch. "Emmie Jo and Joy June."

Caleb was not a happy camper. "What the hell?"

Millie's eyes filled with tears. Through clenched teeth, she said, "I got pregnant that last time under the football stands. Your, uh, swimmers, uh, your boys swam up the creek—"

Caleb wasn't having it. "That's farfetched. Even if it could happen, y'all woulda told me!"

Mille shook her head, sorrow filling her gaze. "No. What good would it do? You'd have tried to marry me, and I couldn't have that."

"So, you had Herman in my place? You married Herman! What kinda sense does that make?"

Millie's hands twisted in front of her. "Pa would have killed you. You are Catholic. You wouldn't have lasted alive long enough to make it to the altar, and I'd be shamed and thrown out with my baby. Herman was there for the taking. I did what I had to do. I kept my baby, well, babies, seeing's how they're twins."

Caleb shook his head, trying to wrap his brain around this news. "Tarnation! I stopped. He couldn't? I had kids? This is too much." Then he asked, "Did Herman know?"

Millie straightened up. "How could he? No, he never had call to doubt they were his."

Caleb looked at her sharply. "Do the twins know?"

She shrugged. "They noticed the likeness to the portrait in Emma Jean's locket. The one with your ma's picture inside."

At the mention of the locket, comprehension dawned on him. "I have that. Skye gave it to me when Auntie Em died."

Millie nodded. "There's a lock of your mother's red hair inside. I was afraid you'd put two and two together, but you never did."

He couldn't stop the bitterness in his tone. "No, I never did."

"You got outta Dodge right quick, too."

Caleb threw his hands up. "Not for years. Not until you decided to cook full time at the Lodge. What else could I do? I couldn't bear to see you every day. And those kids? Well, they got to me." He stepped away from Millie. "Did Aunt Emma Jean know?"

Millie's gaze didn't meet his eyes. "She suspected but left it up to me. I never told her outright. How could I? She knew Pa would shoot you faster than a tick could land on a coon dog's hide on a hot day in July."

"Go away, Millie. G'wan. Git." He drew in a breath and started to walk away.

"Man up, Caleb. For God's sake, be the man Tater thought you were."

"That was low, Millie. About even with findin' out I have kids—fifty years too late."

Millie turned and left him.

Caleb needed two things. A drink and his fiddle. He stomped to his cabin, threw on a clean shirt, combed his hair, splashed on some Savage cologne, and looked in the mirror. He'd put on a black t-shirt that read *I Wrangle Llamas at Le-Conte* in white letters. The outline of a llama was embroidered on a patch over the pocket. He also read the look in his eyes. Dagnabbit, he was angry.

He saw Millie get into her SUV. *She can drive straight to hell. I'm goin' to the bar.*

Things were hoppin' at Bar None. There was no live music that night, but Caleb didn't mind a bit. He had some music in him that he intended to let loose. In one stride, he yanked the cord to the jukebox out of its socket. Dolly Parton's voice stopped cold mid-note. "Jo—"

Caleb picked up his fiddle. He fiddled like he'd never fiddled before. He played all the traditional favorites, and the crowd flooded the dancefloor.

Caleb saw the tall white-haired woman with a trim figure dancin' up a storm. To encourage her gyrations and the other dancers, he launched into *The Devil Went Down to Georgia.* Wally arrived and joined him in the devil's duel.

He spotted Millie, taking a seat at the bar and accepting a beer from her daughter as the devil's dual raged on.

The white-haired woman stopped right in front of Caleb as the tempo picked up. She stopped suddenly—frozen in time—her fingers covering her heart. She took herself a good, solid look at him. Her eyes flickered to his LeConte Llama shirt, then his harmonica and his fiddle. She stared into his eyes, then passed out cold right where she stood, whacking her head against the old oak pickle barrel left over from the revenuer days.

In a heartbeat, Caleb got rid of his instrument and jumped into action to help.

Folks screamed and were pushed aside when Bufford strode in and cleared the dancefloor. "Give her some space. She needs air. Y'all take your seats."

The dude she had been dancin' with cried out. "Jo!"

Joy June ran to the jukebox and plugged it back in. Dolly Parton's unmistakable voice rang out, singing, "Jolene, Jolene, Jolene . . ."

Caleb was checking the woman for injuries when he got the

shock of his life. He wasn't looking at her head now. No, his gaze was focused on the tattoo above her wrist. The same one he'd added to his own wrist when he'd first started hunting for his missing auburn-haired woman. A small llama. The only one he had ever seen besides his belonged to the one woman he spent twenty years trying to find. Jolene. He had found her where he'd first met her. Bar None. When he was no longer looking for her.

"Where the hell have you been, Jolene?"

# CHAPTER NINETEEN: WAITING FOR A GIRL LIKE YOU

Millie's mouth opened in shock. *Jolene? The missing woman? Where's her flaming auburn locks? Her ivory skin? Her emerald eyes? This gal is Caleb's lost love? Is this gal like the one in Dolly's song? Out to take my man? Because she can? Hmph. Ah don't think so. Miss Fancy-free hain't got nuthin' all that special about her. She's rail-thin, and tarnation her hair's stark white. Ain't no competition if you ask me.* Millie shook herself. *Get a grip, gal. This ain't no silly song. This is real life. Still, what's Caleb gonna do now with two gals buzzin' around him?* She thought about it a minute. *I can't let him slip through my fingers again. When Caleb got around to kissin' me, he wasn't just whistling Dixie.* No, he'd meant it, she could tell. She had, too. It felt right. She'd be damned if she'd let him get away again.

Millie watched as Caleb tended to Jolene. Joy June handed a dish towel full of ice from the bar to Caleb. He tried to place it on Jolene's head.

Jolene pushed it away with an impatient swat. "Stop fussing over me. I'm a grown woman. I don't need that, Caleb. I'm fine." She stood, waved Joy June over, and demanded a drink. "Whiskey. Two fingers. The good stuff. Give the bill to Caleb. On second thought, be prepared to bring me another just in case." Jolene moved to take the bottle.

"I can't just leave a bottle with y'all, but I'll keep an eye out for ye."

Then she motioned Caleb into a seat and sank into one herself.

142

Joy June sent everyone else on their way and closed the bar. In the background, the jukebox played *I Saw Her Face*.

Millie headed toward the exit when the others did, nodding to Joy June. But the man who had called out *Jo* did not. She paused at the door and looked back at Caleb.

Caleb's mouth gaped with shock. He shook his head before he spoke. "What the hell happened to yer hair, Jolene? Tarnation, woman! I'd have never found ye. Not with such short white hair."

"Yeah, about that . . ." Jolene began.

Joy June set the shot glass in front of her. Jo finished it faster than Millie thought humanly possible.

Joy June returned to the bar and grabbed the bottle again.

"Jolene?" The dude she had danced with looked confused. "Her name's Jo, but that's all she knows. She's got amnesia."

Jolene huffed. "Not anymore. It's all coming back to me now. Holy Shit! Caleb? Hearing you play that fiddle packed a helluva punch."

The other dude threw up his hands and walked out.

Joy June set another shot on the table for Jolene and retreated, leaving Jolene and Caleb alone.

Millie took the hint and walked out the door.


Jolene felt a little woozy, and her head hurt sumthin' awful. She raised the shot glass and motioned Joy June over. "I need a bigger glass."

Joy June produced one and poured whiskey midway.

Jolene sipped her whiskey as she listened to Caleb talk of all he had done to look for her over the years.

She sighed when he was done. "I'm sorry you looked for me all over the place, but seriously, I had no idea who I was. All I knew was the name *Jo*. I was in a bar and saw the *Coke* sign." She shrugged. "And the rest is history. Coke became my last name. If my memory is correct, then I remember telling you I'm like a tumbleweed. I go where the wind blows. Well, I found myself in Georgia. Not rightly sure how I got there, but I did. Don't make our time together in the past anything more than it was."

Caleb's glance betrayed nothing more than surprise. "And what was that, might I ask?"

"A connection that worked as long as it did and then . . ." She shrugged. "What does it matter now?" She waited a heartbeat, then said in a low choked tone, "I think we lost Bess . . ." She had loved that llama.

Caleb nodded. "Ye did. Frank found Bess the next spring. That's when he told me y'all went missin'. They listed ye as a casualty of the Storm of the Century. No one could find a trace of ye. I felt guilty for fightin' with ye beforehand. Should have insisted ye stay the winter."

"Wasn't your place. It was my call. I was in charge of the llama train. I think I had a flight to catch, too. I have only myself to blame. I hope ye went on with your life."

Caleb shook his head and argued, "You were the train leader, but I had rank."

Jolene shrugged. "I was up for a promotion I never told you about—regional director. I had to go. That's all there is to it. How ye been? You have kids and all that?"

"Yes and no."

"I figured." Jolene looked down at her watch. "Way past closin' time. I don't suppose your wife would like us hooking up again."

"That dog won't hunt. Not in the market for no reunion. I think we said all there was to say."

Jolene nodded.

Caleb climbed into his truck, and just like that, he took himself off.

Jolene mounted her motorcycle and roared into the moonlit night.

# CHAPTER TWENTY: STILL THE ONE

The end-of-season Heritage Hike was coming up, and this time, Millie planned to make sure she was among the alumni doing the climb up Mount LeConte. She phoned Storme and called in a favor. "I need you to talk to your man and have him get me up to LeConte Lodge this weekend, by hook or by crook. Don't care how. Talk to your brother-in-law, Luke, hear? I'll go by whirlybird or horseback, mule or leprechaun. Have them pull any strings they need, but no llama can haul these bones up there. If there's a ranger trick, a logging trail, he can take me as far as possible, but I need to get there in case that honky-tonk ho goes up there tryin' to steal my man."

Millie heard a gulp through the phone, probably because she was usually more cordial to Emma Jean's grandbabies.

"Yes, ma'am," Storme said. "I'll do everything I can to make that happen, but I dunno . . ."

"Don't give me no ifs, ands, buts, or maybes, missy," Millie spoke with no-nonsense sternness. "You and your sister better get me up there. I need to get to Caleb before Jolene does."

Storme sighed. "All you need to do is bake him a sweet potato pie, and you'll have him eating out of your hand, just sayin'."

"Hush your mouth! Ye know the way to a man's heart ain't through his belly — it's way south of there. Even my pie won't cut it. Now, get to it. What are ye waitin' on?"

Storme hung up. Skye had connections through her ranger husband, and Storme's husband was a lawyer. If they couldn't do something, Millie would damn well hike up there herself. She started packing.

Skye phoned Millie a short while later. "I called in all my chips and used every contact we have between us. Meet Junior at Gatlinburg Pigeon Forge Airport at eight o'clock Saturday morning, and he'll get you up there using the scenic helicopter."

Millie drawled. *"Yesss!* The old yeller copter down in Sevierville? Yee Haw! Now that's what I'm talkin' about! Always wanted to try that thing. Good work."

On Friday, Caleb hiked up to the lodge ahead of the folks registered for the annual event. After the event, Caleb would spend his last winter on the mountain. The lodge could house fifty climbers, and he had always looked forward to the end-of-season event. This year he was glad he had an excuse to stay on LeConte. He was still hopping mad at both Millie and Jolene.

Caleb had already talked with the lodge owners, deciding to work there one more winter. He had a lot on his mind and knew the coming winter promised to be bittersweet — especially since Jolene had been found. His thoughts darkened. He needed a distraction, and as usual, he knew he'd find it in the hills.

He figured he could most likely hook up with Jolene again, but . . . *Tarnation . . . Ah just ain't all that into her anymore.* Instead of thinking of Jolene with her still fine-looking trim figure and short white hair, it was another woman with more curves than a mountain switchback that gave him pause. One with a touch of silver laced between her once strawberry hair.

His thoughts shocked him as he hiked the trail. All the way up the mountain, all he did was think of Millie and their last conversation. He was Emmie Jo and Joy June's father. He had kids. And a granddaughter who was having a child. He chuckled. *Everything I ever dreamed of . . . All I have to do is reach out and take it. If Millie will have me. Folks think I was searchin' the hills lookin' for my lost love when really, I was searching for all the wrong reasons. I felt simple guilt and responsibility.* She had been my unfinished business. He had cared about Jolene. But had he really *loved* her? *No. I mighta tried to fool myself, but it weren't love.*

Caleb looked forward to the next day when the Heritage hikers would arrive. He checked the registration list. Only forty-nine names were there. He wondered who the last mystery guest for this year would be.

He went to bed thinking he had three choices. Three paths for his future. Choose between two women who could change his life . . . or remain a bachelor. It was all up to him in the end. The choice was all his. All he had to do was choose which path. Which woman. Or bachelorhood.

# Chapter Twenty-one: All I Need

The helicopter landed on the bald near Myrtle Pointe. Millie thanked the pilot, adjusted her mental bootstraps, grabbed her bags, and hiked the short quarter mile to the LeConte Lodge, beating the other by hours. When she got to the Dining Hall, she welcomed the mountain-grown coffee the staff had prepared for the thirsty crowd. She winked at the server as she sipped the fragrant brew. "The boss in?"

The gal grinned. "Sure is. He's goin' have a full-on fit when he sees you're the *mystery guest*, right?"

Millie raised her fingers to her lips, making the *shh* sign as the woman walked the short distance to the office and announced, "The mystery guest has arrived."


Caleb looked up, surprised. "Already? By gum! Who is it? And how the hell did he get here so fast?"

The staffer shrugged. "Come see for yourself."

Caleb took his wide brim hat off and scratched his head, puzzled. He reviewed his list of possible people, but he was stumped.

Still perplexed, he walked over to the Dining Hall. *Who the hell was it?*

When he walked in the door, he froze at the sight of Millie pulling on an apron.

She gave him a huge smile. "Heard y'all needed a cook for the winter."

Caleb's brain scrambled. "Yep. But . . . The winter? You?

149

Stayin' up here?"

Millie winked. "Yep. I figured I'd apply. See what yer fascination with this place is all about. I have connections with the winter caretaker."

Caleb just stood there, mouth opened, no words forming. Then, "But . . . but . . . how? I mean, we're not married . . ."

"Caleb Weathers, is that a proposal?"

"I reckon it is." Sudden clarity rolled over him like the sun burning through the Smoky Mountain mist. Peace covered him like a thick fleece blanket on a bitterly cold Mount Le-Conte night. His heart filled with a serenity and surety he'd not felt in a long time.

Millie smiled and winked. "About time. I thought you'd never ask. It's high time I make an honest man out of you. Where are your quarters? We gotta get a move on before the preacher gets here."

"We do?"

Millie nodded. "Yep. I figured we're two olives on the same stick, so I asked Father Dale to come up and marry us proper. Reckon this place will make us one fine honeymoon."

And just like that, Caleb ended his bachelor days in a mountain romp with Millie. He had everything he'd ever wanted since childhood — his Millie. Not to mention a ready-made family with kids, grandkids, and even a great-grand-child on the way. *Amazing! I went from a dud to a stud in a heart-beat.*

A breeze rippled through the trees, whispering a barely heard *Wooof* . . . To this day, Caleb would swear it had been Tater's bark of approval.

The End

# OTHER BOOKS BY KATHY KALMAR

The Beach Series
Beyond the Beach Book One
Beyond the Beach Book Two
Beyond the Beach Book Three
Beyond the Beach Book Four
Beyond the Beach Book Five
Back to the Beach Book One
Back to the beach Book Two
Promises on the Beach

The Mountain Series
Mountain Hot
Mountain Christmas
Mountain Skye Prequel to the Weather Girls
Mountain Kiss
Mountain Joy
Mountain Promises
Mountain Holly
Mountain Silver
Mountain Mistletoe
Mountain Bred
Mountain Led
Mountain Wed
Mountain Hookup
Mountain Fever
Mountain Due
Mountain Bachelor

# ABOUT THE AUTHOR

Kathy Kalmar, born in Detroit, Michigan, lives with Larry, her husband of four decades. Lately, she feels her life has recovered from the bad country song-like life because her Smoky Mountain Tops Round House is now rebuilt from the 2016 Chimney Tops II Wildfire. Her current residence is enlarged by four feet for their new puppy, Valentina. She loves to read and write contemporary romance novels.

Currently, she is writing her next book. Meanwhile she remains fond of hot tubbing, chocolate, and sipping wine and mai tais whether at home, Waikiki, Cape Cod, or Tennessee. Y'all come back, hear? Aloha and Mahalo.